FICTION SOUTH / FICTION NORTH

EDITED BY COLLINS & MILAZZO

RIDGEFIELD
PRESS

FICTION SOUTH / FICTION NORTH
Copyright © 1991 Ridgefield Press, editors, authors, photographers and artists.
All Rights Reserved.
First Printing, January 1992.
Library of Congress Catalog Card Number: 91-90447.
I.S.B.N.: 0-9631022-0-6.
Typesetting by Moses Rodin, Gallery Graphics, Tallahassee, Florida.
Printed by Rose Printing Company, Inc., Tallahassee, Florida.
Cover illustration: Dennis Hopper, *Double Standard*, ca. 1961-67.

CONTENTS

CREDITS AND ACKNOWLEDGEMENTS

Pamela Ball's *The Centipede of Attraction* is an excerpt from a novel in progress, and is published by permission of the author; Owen Goodwyne's story, *Deadeye*, is previously unpublished, and appears by permission of the author; Barry Handberg's *A Limited Response* is an excerpt from an unpublished novel (ca. 1983), and appears by permission of the author; Ed Marsicano's story, *Roberto de Castro*, is previously unpublished, and appears by permission of the author; Bob Shacochis' short story, *Lord Short Shoe Wants the Monkey* (1982), is reprinted from his first collection of stories, *Easy in the Islands* (1985), by permission of Crown Publishers, Inc., Penguin Books and the author; Gary Scott White's *The Square Root of Fun (A Surd in Three Parts)* is an excerpt from an unpublished novel, and appears by permission of the author. The excerpt actually constitutes Part II of the novel, and is entitled "Such."

Michael Cunningham's "Clare" is an excerpt from his novel, *A Home at the End of the World* (1990), and is reprinted by permission of Farrar Straus Giroux and the author; Gary Indiana's *The Fever* is an excerpt from a novel in progress, and is published by permission of the author; Patrick McGrath's *Spider* (1990) is an excerpt from his novel by the same name, and is published by permission of Poseidon Press and the author; Eileen Myles's *Robert Mapplethorpe Picture* is previously unpublished, and appears by permission of the author; Lynne Tillman's *The Break* is an excerpt from a novel in progress, and is published by permission of the author; Wendy Walker's story, *Laüstic*, is from a new collection, *Stories Out of Omarie*, and is previously unpublished, and appears by permission of the author.

The photographs of the authors are by the following, with their permission: Pamela Ball by Stuart Riordan, Bob Shacochis by Carole Patterson, Michael Cunningham by Elena Seibert, Gary Indiana by Elinor Veshes, Eileen Myles by Bob Berg, Lynne Tillman by Ioni Laibaros, and Patrick McGrath by Orshi Drozdik.

The photo of Collins & Milazzo is by Timothy Greenfield-Sanders. The cover photograph is by Dennis Hopper. The logo for Ridgefield Press was especially created by Liz Trovato for Ridgefield Press.

THE EDITORS

FOREWORD

Fiction South / Fiction North is the first book published by Ridgefield Press. It contains writings by Pamela Ball, Michael Cunningham, Owen Goodwyne, Barry Handberg, Gary Indiana, Ed Marsicano, Patrick McGrath, Eileen Myles, Bob Shacochis, Lynne Tillman, Wendy Walker and Gary Scott White. *Fiction South / Fiction North* functions to inaugurate not only the birth of a publishing house but, it is to be hoped, the rebirth of the Book itself as an active and effective cultural instrument.

Ridgefield Press is a non-profit organization based in Tallahassee, Florida, and New York City, dedicated to publishing books in the fields of literature, art and the various crafts.

Modeling itself after The Hogarth Press, founded by Virginia Woolf and the Bloomsbury group in London in 1917, as well as the Arts and Crafts movement led by Gustav Stickley in America (which was begun in nineteenth-century England by such artists and philosopher-critics as John Ruskin and William Morris), it is the intention of Ridgefield Press to create a distinguished link between the practical and the intellectual, the aesthetical and the social, and between local and international culture. Ridgefield Press was founded and is edited by Patricia Collins and Richard Milazzo.

Ridgefield Press derives its name from the farm in Tallahassee, Florida, once owned by Rosalie and Ralph Potts, aunt and uncle to Patricia Collins. Ridgefield Press is located at The Cottage at Ridgefield, in what was the guest house on a small segment of the farm, and now home to Patricia Collins and Richard Milazzo. The press was conceived originally as a homage to Rosalie Potts, whose appreciation for the crafts was in the deepest tradition of life in America during a time long gone by. Together, Rosalie and Ralph Potts bred and cross-bred innumerable varieties of camellias of extraordinary beauty and distinction, which flourish and may still be seen today at Ridgefield. Besides her interest in furniture and gardening, Aunt Rosie (as she was known to her family and friends) had built by hand, from limestone indigenous to the area, the hearth in her home at Ridgefield, picking the stones one by one from the pasture just outside her door. The fireplace and house are still standing, and are part of the home that Emma Lou and James Brogdon, sister and brother-in-law to Patricia Collins, make at Ridgefield. Living testimony of Rosalie's deep feelings and love for the land and this part of the country as a whole, was provided in the prose poem, "Ridgefield," that Rosalie Potts left behind after her death, and which was only recently discovered by Emma Lou in a box of old things she found in the attic.

RIDGEFIELD
by Rosalie G. Potts

I *Pond Road*

Eastward out, toward north, winding down clay-banked, oak-covered, long-traveled trail, Apalachee trod, wagon-rolled clay road, over plank road, hard road; wheels driven still—the same route.   Left, off to a sideroad, "Potts Road," clay-packed, pond-banked—to either side. Cutting through marsh-grass-filled shallow waters, plied with plants underneath; in spring—green blades protruding, pods pushing to surface stalked by water-long legged birds; stub perched by smaller birds—hovering on beating wings—drifting silently, the spaces of this remanent sanctuary; feathers wafting down as dusk—late summer sun—purple through haze rising, fog sifting off the maze of mauve pickerel-weed blossoms, blooming late evening's color—blazing in morning's bright rise.

II *Hill Rising*

Ruts grooved in the dry crusted color, grinding dust blanketing behind. Rain over, leaving streams and rivulets, rushing down, draining hillsides. The climb begins up around a curve—past the cattails, shrub-edge of the white titi, sweet wax myrtle; dewberry vines tenacle across and under fallen leaf mulch, mold—to the brown mantle and mass-green—

under oak, needle and cone covering; smilax, briar, all manner of weeds—wild undergrowth thinning, spreading out in even-cropped pastures, grass tufted, covered by red round heads of clover poking up out of root and runner.

III *Ridgefield*

In the midst of rolling land, atop the mound risen up; towering tall in the horizon from distance viewed. Looking south to one more rise and fall before the gradual dropping off—down miles—the Gulf's edge, coast winding, swamp-drained shallows deepening to blue as the sky overhead. Here pristine pines, tall and straight, lofty oaks, white-black, sassafras, hickory, and tulip trees; thickets of wild plum, dogwood, redbud, down to a buckeye clustered in rows of azaleas—to the persimmon bush; all manner of flowering shrubs; across the crest, camellias spread, and spring's sweet aroma fills the day with daffodils pushing yellow pedals of sun up out of winter's dormant leaf-covered earth. Bare limbs break almost with sound of buds bending to leaves—bows catch the wind and hold the rain—spears of life itself.

Across the cattle gap and acre, winding on up the hill—this world of its own; the palm from which pastures finger out, cattle graze; ground rolling down to an edge of wood, covered with grape vine—twisting up trunks, holding limbs bound, taper out, back and bend toward the ground; open fence-posted wrapping round, up to the water trough, salt lick, collard-sized garden and pear hanging down—mock orange-thorn jutting branches, ivy covering, catching limbs, swing out in dark leaf, thick green.

IV *Remembering*

Here, when walked to the edge of the field, moon's rise can be seen climbing up over the hills; sun's red setting flashes as fire, through silhouettes and shadows of broom sage. Squirrel chased, bird flown and sung, rabbit run and quail covey—nest—in grass straw bundles; doves coo, black birds call, crows caw, and rooster crow can be heard from the houses scattered down along the ridge. Hill, where winds rage, and rip leaves asunder, lightening's thunder crashes the silence of sun—summer storm. Then the calm, and almost still of night except for crickets chirping, and owl's occasional hoot. Now, the sap running a sweet taste of honey to the hungry limbs, roots hold, digging deep to quench the leaf's thirst.

Limbs grow old, rot, break and fall; become firewood to place upon the hearth to light and watch the flame, feel the warmth in fall's cool evening. Dogs bark, race and run to greet you; days amble on, one after another, one into another until seasons replenish, replace and finally rest in time's own pace; nature nourishing itself in year's soft tumble. The ridge of fields—here from the pine's pinnacle to the underside of the lowest leaf, much to discover, come to know, to look for and see—dappled things, the life-giving of it all; seasons echo one into another—God-given, death-taken, one for the other.

Ridgefield Press was originally conceived also to enable the publication of the work of little-published or unpublished authors in Tallahassee and surrounding areas, long-known to the editors both as writers and friends, some of whom have worked as lawyers, teachers, office-workers and day-laborers, and all of whom have been thoroughly devoted to their writing for years. To this group, we added the writings of one or two better known writers. Thus, came into being *Fiction South*. About a year later, the editors saw no reason not to extend the book to writers from the North, mostly New York City, given that the editors also live and work there, and also because they know a great many writers there, both known and lesser known, all of whom, however, are quite deserving. Thus, was added *Fiction North*.

In effect, the title, *Fiction South / Fiction North,* is a working trope and does not purport to function as a sociological or anthropological study. It merely provides examples, we hope excellent ones, of the kind of fiction being written today, both in the South and in the North, but it does not intend to make a definitive statement about the genetic make-up of the writers who live and work in these parts of the country. In fact, many of these writers have travelled quite a bit, as is the traditional habit of writers, and some of them have also lived and/or worked in Germany, England, Hawaii, Cuba and the Caribbean, for prolonged periods of time. It would also be hard to generalize about the kinds of fiction documented in this book. There are almost as many different styles and sets of concerns in the anthology as there are authors. There are in the book examples of the new 'gothic' writing, personalism, magical realism and 'language' writing, as well as writings that are characterized, on the one end, by a new kind of high melodrama, and, on the other, by a certain kind of deadpan facticity. Not to mention other kinds that promise still further developments. To say the least, the conceit, here, in this working model, is as much arctic as it is tropical. So much for Tennessee Williams, Stéphane Mallarmé and Herman Melville.

We express our appreciation to the twelve authors, without whose contributions *Fiction South / Fiction North* would not have been possible. We would also like to thank the photographers for their portraits of the writers, Dennis Hopper for the cover photograph, and Liz Trovato for the creation of the logo for Ridgefield Press. In the case of previously published works, thanks are also due to the publishers and authors who extended their permission to Ridgefield to reprint excerpts from their books.

Special thanks are also due to Debi Baber, David Linn, Bonnie Williams, Robin Hassler, Deborah Kearny, Susan Williams, Jim Murley, Emma Lou and James Brogdon, Craig Adcock, Howard Johnson, and Nicholas Howey, without whose help, dedication and vision, Ridgefield Press would simply not exist. Some of these individuals, as well as others, helped to organize the fund raiser in November 1990 to benefit Ridgefield Press, and for this they, as well as all those who made a financial contribution to Ridgefield Press, must also be thanked.

Thanks also go to Charles Bernstein, Bob Shacochis, Catfish, Gary Indiana and Tyler Turkle for their special support.

PATRICIA COLLINS AND RICHARD MILAZZO
NEW YORK CITY AND LIVE OAK ISLAND, FLORIDA, JUNE 1991

xiii

FICTION SOUTH

PAMELA BALL

OWEN GOODWYNE

BARRY HANDBERG

ED MARSICANO

BOB SHACOCHIS

GARY SCOTT WHITE

from *The Centipede of Attraction*

Pamela Ball

In Hilo, there were dead sharks hanging on hooks under the rafters of the small wooden buildings. Within days the line of grey flesh multiplied, and when no one was looking, people put their hands out and touched the hard, rubbery skin. The blood pooled on the ground and the fishermen gathered in circles around the edges of the blood and later their slippers left tracks down the sidewalk, mixing the blood of one dead shark with another. The fishing supply store ran out of gaffs and marlin hooks and rope, and the shoe store ran out of the high wooden getas that would keep people's feet away from the blood. It was like nothing I'd ever seen.

Well, I didn't know. I looked at the line of sharks and at the people milling around with tape measures flashing in their hands. It all had the outside shape of a celebration, if you stood far enough away. If you stood far enough away almost anything would take a shape, even the things that took people away or brought them back. My ex-husband Amos hadn't ever come back to the Big Island, but even after fifteen years everywhere I turned he was the cause of what I saw. I didn't know if I was more possessed by his absence than by the man himself.

It was all due to the boy. I couldn't even get used to the idea of the boy, never mind that he wasn't a boy, really, but a young man named Bradley, who was my ex-husband's stepson.

A week ago, Bradley had come to the Big Island, and had looked me up. He was proud of the fact that he'd found me; I didn't point out that any fool could have found me; I'd been in one town my whole life. I wasn't the one who'd left.

Bradley paced around, amazed at himself for being on the Big Island. He kept saying so this is the place where Amos was born. Bradley was dressed in safari clothes. The clothes of an explorer.

That was when I relented a little bit, realizing he was just a silly kid adjusting his man-sized belt, bunching up his long pants. He was in costume. Still, I was irritated that he was so large; so fully grown. The idea of him would have been much easier to deal with in some smaller, less finished form.

He said he needed work, so I drove him down to the harbor in my old Ford truck that had to be left running or kickstarted, and I sat in the cab with the engine idling, pointing out different boats that I knew were hiring.

It was early in the morning, and the flat side of the mountain behind us was a soft pink, the same color that was reflected on the water, and by the time I'd rolled a cigarette the water had turned metal-colored, the rain started, and Bradley was scampering from boat to boat. The first boat probably would have hired him, except for the weirdness of his clothes. I could have gone down to the dock myself, and introduced him and gotten him on the very first boat, but there were things I just wouldn't do. It was bad enough that the kid was staying at my house.

By the time I'd rolled and smoked another cigarette he'd found a boat that would hire him, and turned to wave at me in the car. He looked like a giant windmill, with his long arms pumping away, and I realized that he wasn't going to quit waving until I waved back, and so after a minute I did. The last time I looked at him, he was halfway out the harbor in a flag line boat, his hat cocked to one side and securely fastened under his chin.

Later, they said that he'd worked hard for a haole boy from the Mainland, that even if he seemed a little silly, he'd kept up with the work. Later they said a lot of things, but on the way back in, on his very first day, Bradley decided to jump off the boat before they came around the breakwater.

Everyone on the boat warned him not to do it, but he was over the side so quickly that they didn't have time to tell him why. After a day of their boat being followed by sharks, they didn't think they had to warn him. He yelled from the water that he'd swim in from there, his arm waving to all the men who were gesturing at him to come back, but he was from somewhere with lakes, not an ocean, and the boat was too far out.

Before they could turn the boat around to pick him up, they saw the fin of a shark coming from the opposite direction, heading for him faster than they were, with their engine in full throttle. He had his arm up, waving; he never saw what was behind him, and his arm twirled in the air as the shark attacked, and he yelled, just once.

The captain of the boat came to my house, and told me that Bradley was dead. I wasn't even over being jealous of him yet. He even had my last name. Merriweather.

"How am I supposed to feel?" I asked the captain.

"Hey, I don't know, Hope. I don't think I'm feeling anything at *all,*" he said, "but look." He held his hand out and it quivered, and we both stared at it, stupidly, until he put it down again.

I had to call my ex-husband Amos and tell him that his stepson was dead. I sat in front of the phone, not wanting to call him, waiting for it to ring instead, for Amos to have miraculously been told by someone else. I hadn't talked to Amos in years, except in my mind. I put my words in his mouth, mostly having him beg for forgiveness. Sometimes I did forgive him, and sometimes I didn't.

But the phone didn't ring, and when I called him I knew his voice right away. All I let him say was hello, and then I said "Bradley's dead, Amos, and I'm so sorry." I didn't know how to warm people up to bad news. All I could do was squeeze my eyes shut and jump.

"Why?" Amos said, after a moment.

Which why, I wondered. Why was I sorry, or why was Bradley dead.

"Loss of blood," I said, finally, thinking of Bradley's arms waving. "He died from loss of blood."

"What the hell does that mean?" Amos whispered, and then I told him all of it, all except the scream, and the waving.

I wanted to leave it at that, get off the phone, but Amos wanted more from me. I hadn't heard him crying like that since he'd left me, fifteen years earlier, for Bradley's mother. I couldn't figure out why he didn't just hang up and go do his crying with Bradley's mother. It seemed like my life was turning into some immense sit-down dinner that I kept trying to excuse myself from, but somewhere, someone was always trying to make me finish everything on my plate. "No thank you, I've had this dish before," just didn't work. Hearing Amos cry was like sitting down to that god-awful dinner again. I was already full, but here we were still on the first course.

Amos was incoherent for days. He called me constantly from his home in California, but all he did was play thirty questions once he got me on the line. He gave the answers, I was supposed to guess the questions.

"I should have been there," he said.

I wondered how far back he'd like to set that clock. Then he blamed Bradley, which was more to the point. I blamed the other world, the one running alongside this one.

It seemed I was right, because the next day Amos came up with an idea that made his voice clear on the line. I remembered that tone, and it made me nervous.

He decided to put a bounty on sharks. Ten dollars per foot. Amos still knew a lot of people in Hilo, and before the end of the day he'd called around, and the word was out. Fishermen started coming into town from as far away as Kona and down the mountain from Kamuela, to make extra money. A few days later Amos called me back, raising the price on pregnant sharks.

"Now, why didn't I think of that," I said, and from then on I quit answering the phone.

I drove slowly down the streets in Hilo, the town that Amos and I had both been raised in, the town that seemed to have shrunk down since the boy died. A young boy dying made me feel suddenly old, as if my forty-five-year old body had stiffened overnight. Even my hands on the steering wheel looked like someone else's hands. They were too gnarled and veiny to be mine.

In the park I drove under the monkeypod trees that threw dark shadows of lace onto the sky, and I looked up and thought of reefs, of dense clumps of coralhead, of places that were safe and places that weren't. I'd always thought it was what you knew that would kill you. I was getting tired of holding all the wrong answers.

I tried not to be, but I was drawn down to the bay along with everyone else. I idled in the loading zone that no one had ever dared ask me to move out of, not even when I was an underage kid driving my father's old Nash, the only Nash on the Big Island, through my

6

marriage to Amos in a beat up old Valiant, and definitely not now, when I was forty-five years old in a Ford pick-up.

I rolled a cigarette and watched the boats, and the point farther out, where the water turned metal-colored, where the boy had died, and I thought surely a landscape must be worn down by what happens in it.

I wanted to think of Bradley as a man now that he was dead. I wanted to remember something particular about him. The way he carried himself, whether or not he was at ease in the world. The truth was, I'd hardly looked at him. I'd tried so hard not to see him. He had a safari tinge to every piece of clothing he had, hands that moved like startled birds, and a face that was almost too unmarked. That wasn't much, but I saw no reason to spend a lot of time on a boy whose mother had taken Amos from me.

Bradley's mother had come to the Big Island as a tourist. She was staying in a fancy hotel, and she had a lot of money, not that I thought that was the deciding factor, but it didn't hurt. Amos must have liked the idea of being paid to walk away from one life and start another. Sometimes Amos would come home and I was wiping noses or making butterfly bandages and he'd look around as if he'd walked into the wrong house.

One afternoon, Bradley's mother went into the elevator of her fancy hotel and got stuck between floors. Amos was called in on his emergency beeper, and I couldn't ever hear one of those things going off without having the feeling that someone's life was getting ready to change completely.

Later, I'd asked Amos what he'd said to keep her from panicking, while he repaired the elevator.

He shrugged. "The usual things," he said. "You'll be fine."

"What else?"

"We're doing everything we can, or just hang on. The real trick is to say them one at a time."

He was the first person she saw after the hour it took him to fix the elevator, and granted, I gave Amos credit, he had beautiful dark hair the color of split-open coal, and long boatshaped eyes, and wherever he went, he was the center of attention. The centipede of attraction, I used to call him.

Then I felt what it was that I had named him.

Still, she seemed like some kind of gosling, hatching after her hour in the elevator, and following forever the first face she saw, which was Amos'.

She started calling him at our home. Postponed her trip back to the Mainland. Had her nanny come out to take care of Bradley, so she could concentrate on the job of getting Amos.

Amos talked to her on the phone, she had our number by the day after her ordeal. She talked to him about how important it was to be able to reach the one person who knew what she'd been through, while Amos would roll his eyes at me during their whole conversation. Then he'd get off the phone and we'd laugh about the possibility of a reward, since she was so rich. Then all of a sudden there wasn't that much to laugh about.

It wasn't as if all those memories were suddenly on me again. I'd never even put them down. I watched the fishermen and wondered if they found it possible to move closer to the boy when they killed a shark. I understood vengeance as well as anyone, but once it started it was never enough.

My friend Alapai was down at the dock, getting ready to go out. I parked on the hill and turned my engine off, and ran past the ice house, flagging down his boat before it left the pier.

Alapai cut across the channel towards me in his boat with the sampan hull favored on the Big Island. It was a shape I'd known all my life, a shape I was at ease in, as calm as I was when parked in the loading zone.

I'd known Alapai since I was a kid, and I didn't have to explain anything, just jumped on board when he came up next to the pier, and held tightly to the fishing pole that he gave me.

To attract sharks he poured a gallon of slaughterhouse blood over the side of the boat. I was basically an eye for an eye kind of person, but that was before I saw the blood spreading in the water like a reef, like the canopy of a monkeypod tree. After awhile it seemed like I was no longer smelling the sharp rusty scent of blood, that instead it was smelling me. It was on me like the scent of a dog, a smell that rose up off the wet streets and followed me home and stayed in the room with me.

BALL

The smell of the blood mixed in with the smell of the diesel engine. I felt sick. It was the wrong boat ride to be throwing up on. I wanted to remember something big, a sign beyond that of the rim of a rubber bucket that I was heaving my guts into. Backbone, I told myself. Stamina. I reminded myself that I'd never thrown up on a boat in my entire life; I'd practically grown up on boats. Then I went down below and on my knees I memorized the rim of that bucket.

Alapai took the boat farther out, where most of the other boats were. It looked like a fishing tournament in full swing, and everyone was festive, making money off Amos. I never let him send me money, not even child support. I knew it was her money, and I wasn't going to let him ease his conscience that way.

The waves turned into swells and the color of the sea went from metal to turquoise, and when we were far enough out, to navy blue. I felt like a complete fool, not even knowing if I was on the boat for the boy or for Amos, and I looked back at the island whose shape was tattooed across my memory, and Amos' memory too, because the island wasn't a thing you could let go of. Somewhere in the corner of whatever he was seeing now, in the Mainland, there was this same dark shape. Why else would his stepson have come? I wondered if Amos had told the boy much about me. I looked down at the deck of the boat, looked down my long tan legs and my feet in rubber zoris. I've still got great legs, I thought, the same legs that I had when Amos was here.

My line started whining, running out so fast that by the time I scrambled into the chair it had taken out over two hundred yards. I got nervous and almost gave my seat up to Alapai, but then I stayed where I was, and Alapai pretended that he hadn't seen me waver.

I braced my feet against the side of the boat and worked the shark. I knew it was a shark, because I just wasn't prepared to go through that kind of effort for some damn fish, not even ahi. After about twenty minutes Alapai came over and massaged my shoulders, and I felt like a damn tourist in a marlin tournament, and that made me laugh. Once I started laughing everything was funny, there was no stopping but Alapai just ignored it, let me wind up and play out like the fishing line and when I was finally quiet he started talking, filling in the space that was left.

9

"Sometimes when I come out here, you know what I remember?"

I couldn't look at him, I was working so hard on trying not to laugh.

"That time when we were six or seven years old and we went around town and made all the men lift up their shirts so that we could see whether they had a shark jaw buried in the middle of their back, you remember that?"

I smiled, and he put a baseball hat on my head. I was getting tired, especially in my lower back.

After Alapai had gone to the other end of the boat I thought of that god who was a shark, who came on land in the shape of a man, always a beautiful man, but he couldn't hide the shark mouth in his back. There were things that you carried from one world to the next. While some men had laughed, and pulled their shirts up voluntarily for us, pleased to be thought of as a god, others refused, and we'd follow them home and spy on them. We had to wait for them to go swimming, or catch them doing yardwork on a hot day.

I was still working the line, slowly gaining a little, when Alapai turned the boat around and headed back in toward the island and the swells disappeared into waves and the water turned metal-colored again. It seemed a long journey for what turned out to be just one small shark. I heard Alapai yell for the captain's gaff, and then he leaned over the side of the boat, and the gun went off.

He grunted as the motionless shark was gaffed and brought in over the side of the boat.

After congratulating me, they left me alone with the shark. I watched it for a few minutes, wondering who I could ask now to tell me how to feel about it, when all of a sudden the shark flipped itself over next to where I was standing. I jumped up into the hold and on my hands and knees I scrambled up on my feet and turned to look at it. Once again the shark was still, its eye motionless. I found Alapai's baseball bat tucked behind the tackle box. I pulled it out and stepped over to the shark and clubbed it on the head again and again until I was sure it was dead. Then I clubbed it some more, and the eye spilled out the way the stomach lining fell like fabric from the sharks that were hung up on hooks in the town.

It was as scary looking dead as it had been alive, with its fake-looking skin and face wound up tight like I'd seen on certain people when they were getting ready to do something entirely crazy. Alapai congratulated me on my mighty swing, while ignoring my bloody knees and panicked breathing. He predicted our welcome back at the dock, and I wondered if the whole point of a bounty was to show you that you didn't know anything about yourself or anyone else. If so, I'd learned it. Once, I'd thought it would be as simple as finding a jaw buried in someone's back.

We came into the harbor as it was getting dark, and the lights were turned on along the dock. I was relieved that most of the people had gone home. I stepped out of the boat and onto the hosed-down dock, with pools of light shining on the wood. The harbormaster took the shark and hung it up under a spotlight.

I went back up the hill to my truck before they started gutting it. At home, I finally slept through an entire night.

What I woke up to was Amos calling from the Mainland. He thought interest might be lagging, so he decided to raise the price per foot. I pictured him standing on a mountain somewhere, making god-like gestures with his fists full of Bradley's mother's money.

Within days, a whole hierarchy had been established, from the person who measured the length of each shark, down to the man who had the job of gutting them. I had no idea how he had been picked. He was a truck gardener. I'd never even seen him near a boat, though I recognized his new prestige, I could see it in the small of his back, and in the way that he shuffled in his fake leather slippers with the small toes hanging out each side, lightly grazing the sidewalk. Each time he gutted a shark, the crowd went into automatic pilot while buoys and beer cans and clorox bottles spilled out with the stomach. I'd already caught my shark, and my job now, I realized suddenly, was to witness it.

All the men were dry from the waist up. I saw each man's strong back in the center of a circle of people, and though I was too far away to hear, I watched their hands telling the same story that every other pair of hands had been telling. A new boat came in, just minutes after the first, and the center changed as the people moved onto the next group, discarding their previous excitement the way spectators left the scene of an accident that didn't pan out.

There could have been a shave ice stand, things were that weirdly festive. The fish were dead, but everything else was fresh. People talked more than they had in years, rival shopkeepers nodded over the same dead shark. Kids on bicycles rode through the blood with their feet held out to the sides, and the blood spraying out beneath them.

Each fisherman wanted to kill that first shark, the one which had attacked the boy, and then waiting for the fish to be gutted, each man had a look of relief when the stomach opened and it didn't turn out that way.

I went home. I stood naked in front of the mirror and brushed my long coarse hair. I looked at my body, registering the changes that had taken place over the last fifteen years. I looked like I'd been through it, and I had. It was better, I decided, than looking untouched like what's-her name, better than looking like a vacant building that no one had even moved into.

I put my clothes back on, and went out again. I circled the wet streets in Hilo like a teenager, eating from an okazu plate on my lap, with a six pack of beer in the backseat. I drove up to Volcano and sat for a while in the mist, pretending that there was nothing going on down in Hilo, but even up in Volcano the mist was shark-colored.

I realized suddenly that I'd always thought we'd work something out, even though Amos' idea of the perfect life was like one of those drive-in movie theatres that they had on the Mainland, where there were three screens and three movies running simultaneously, and all a person like Amos had to do was turn his head and he'd be in another movie, another life, and the one he'd turned away from would keep on going. He believed that it would turn out the same whether he was in it or not.

I came back down from Volcano, and headed straight for the harbor. There still weren't any parking places. There were pickups backed in sideways and the sharks that had been dead for a day were hauled off in the beds of some trucks while the newly dead sharks were being carefully unloaded off the beds of other trucks. Not even the fishermen knew why the newly dead sharks should be treated with any more care. It was just past training, the kind none of us could get away from.

I parked in the loading zone, which was turning out to be the safest place to be on the whole island. I got out my papers and rolled a couple of cigarettes, lining them up neatly across the dash, and watched a cop walk back and forth in front of my truck, getting himself all wound up about parking in the loading zone. He was new to the police force, and I could tell that he wasn't sure whether I mattered or not. I pulled the chopstick out of my bun, and my long white hair fell around my shoulders. Read that, I thought.

I looked at that cop, and thought of Alapai's story about the shark god. What if that god had a twisted sense of tradition? What if he came on land as a young haole cop from the Mainland? I wondered how the cop would feel about lifting up his shirt, but then we were both distracted by a boat coming into the harbor.

I didn't recognize either the boat or the men. One of them held up three fingers. Three sharks. The other one kept making triangular shapes with his arms. He looked hysterical, and I realized I'd seen enough, more than enough.

They'd found Bradley's body, what was left of it. The harbormaster almost carried the one man who'd been making triangle shapes off the boat, sitting him down on an upside bucket on the dock. Someone else put a beer in his hand but he never even lifted his head. Then they all had beers, the whole crowd was drinking and the people gathered and broke over the three men, like waves. I saw it. I could have not looked, but I did and I saw them holding what looked like grey wood gone soft in the water, and I could not take my eyes off it, that was the truth.

Even for people who'd not looked, Bradley would be remembered in ways that would give no comfort. The children in town would remember him as a haole boy from the Mainland who hadn't listened. The children themselves were sick of listening, and followed those fishermen who didn't lecture them on safety, jostling to be nearest to those men who were making their own wide circles of blood. The kids were having the time of their lives, though I imagined that at night their dreams were something physical that they had to pass through.

I decided I'd never forgive Amos, but that wasn't exactly a new thought. By my reckoning, Amos had a bill the size of which he could never pay off, and sometimes I thought maybe I liked it that way. Watching the sharks and the men and the wet money changing hands, I thought how much I still wanted him.

Since the bounty started I felt like I was living in a dark underwater place, in an elevator shaft, in the center of the earth. I could hear a voice and it was Amos giving me words one by one, like a rope let down by inches, words that might have worked in one world but not in the one I was in. I didn't know the words that would save any of us. But how many choices did we have? I was waiting for words to fall the way I'd seen flowers, once, over a burial at sea. They were vanda orchids and they were all falling separately.

Deadeye

Owen Goodwyne

Then was 1912. I was twenty. It was back before I changed my name to Beaufort Stratton from Robert Townsend. It was back some fifty years ago, I was shot between the eyes when I stepped between two men in an unfair fistfight at a rattlesnake round-up in Cordele, Georgia. People were eating barbecue. Those that weren't, were standing in line for it, and the derringer's bullet came from a life-saving angle. It ricocheted off my lucky skull and came out under my left eye. Though I could see out of it again before three months later—about the time my oldest child, Charlie Boy, who's with me tonight and feeling good at Luther's Tavern, my favorite bar in north Jacksonville—about the time Charlie Boy was born, I could see out the eye again but I permanently lost the ability to move it.

That eye became my calling card for combat. Day to day, hour upon hour, the straightjacketed eye preached to me that I was bad all the way through, mean to the gills, always hoping, itching for trouble. Something rather simple like being shortchanged when buying papers and tobacco, such would cock my head and aim that eye at whoever it was for sure wanted a verbal lashing together with a knuckle sandwich.

The only man who ever tried to stick me with the nickname of "Deadeye," he got his balls kicked in before being strangled to death. It was 1920. It was the eve of the Fourth of July. Can't swear, but I remember it as being a Saturday. It was after the Herbert Cypress Company's six-to-six shift in one of the Okefenokee Swamp's remaining forests. It was suppertime and thirty of us loggers—some railroad men—occupied the Green Frog Restaurant in the heart of the swamp, between the much-used wharf and the much-used tram line built up on pilings, on Billy's Island.

"JUMP—JUMP—JUMP," some cried.

"GET A CHAIR. GET A CHAIR," others shouted. All
wanted to help young Tommy Joe Hancock from Valdosta. He was
on his tiptoes trying to give a sip of rum, made from cane grown on
Cowhouse Island, to the stuffed black bear filling up a corner.

Like shooing flies, six or seven fans only shooed at what we
jacks called the "Primitive Baptist heat." Must've been. Must've
been the tobacco smoke keeping swamp mosquitoes, promised by
the Herbert Company to be non-malarial, from flying in the side
door that might as well have been propped open since it led outside
to the privy. Loud? It was loud. There was talk of the goodness of
the cheesegrits and of the fingerlings, the catfish pulled up by pole,
Ardmore said, out of the mahogany waters of nearby Minnie's
Lake. There was talk, eager talk, concerning tomorrow's holiday,
one of four when the crosscut saws in the Okefenokee are quiet.
Heated talk, banter there was, over the government's idea for a
barge canal that Hartsfield's ugly buddy was saying would drain the
swamp away from the Gulf-feeding Suwannee and into the Atlantic. "By way of," he said after a spate of cursing, "the winding,
good-tasting St. Marys River." And there was talk, talk of the Davis
boy—eleven years old was all he was—killed yesterday by a small
but powerful locomotive pulling flat cars of cypress to the mill in
Herbertville, killed because he knew no better than to use the
elevated tram line to keep from getting his knees wet while crossing
a lily-padded prairie.

It was so loud inside the Green Frog that evening, that
coming-up Fourth of July, I didn't get to hear the swamp come to
life. Didn't get to hear the gators grunting, bellowing like bulls at
the sunset.

"Sugarfoot," I say.

He's my crosscut mate. Sometimes I let him be my buddy.
He's passing the hushpuppy platter and the Louisiana hot sauce to
Nelson, a jack with a pale forehead and the jack with the most
whiskers. Sugarfoot's talking in a whirlwind, bragging about the
swap of his two otter pelts that got him the deal of the decade, got
him a quart of Shuford's oak-aged corn whiskey. And he goes on
to tell us ignoramuses at the table who'll listen, he tells us where the
womenfolk now like for us to part our hair and the right length for

our whiskers. Then he gets up to give a sampler of the bunny hop that he says he's going to dance tonight in Waycross until his legs drop off.

"Sugarfoot!" He pays me no mind, talking instead like a chicken runs with its head wrung off.

I stomp on the toe of his brogan.

"JESUS H. CHRIST."

"Remember what I told ya on Bugaboo Island this morning." While counting cypress for the superintendent, I told him to keep his trap shut about cavorting in Waycross, especially at the Expresso Club. "I'd hate like hell to have to feed your tongue, Sugarfoot, to some ole hungry stray dog."

I'm thirsty.

I'm going back to the present, to 1966, to get myself a drink. Going there will cost me though—make me again seventy-four years old.

Charlie Boy is in the john. He's been in there quite a while. I don't think my son's drunk so much beer that he's in there throwing up. I think he's drunk just enough beer that he's in there having to piss a very long time.

Luther, the proprietor, is a good buddy. He's a youngster though—Charlie Boy's age—fifty-four, fifty-five years old. Luther sits on a stool at the end of a curved bar where he can keep an eye on his five or six customers. I wait. I look at the clock. It's almost nine. It's a Friday evening. It's the end of October. It's—I'm feeling fine. There now. Finally. Luther's magazine drops. His eyebrows rise. I signal back: yeh, another round.

I told Charlie Boy ten years ago. I remember well that it was ten years ago because I was still toting my tools down at the shipyard. I told Charlie Boy ten years ago that I killed a man but I didn't tell him the cocksucker from Waycross was a Ware County deputy sheriff. I told Charlie Boy—I told him not too long after that day in the yard when we put two and two together and figured out I was Charlie Boy's pa. Pleased. I was pleased to learn that a mighty fine leaderman was my son. I told Charlie Boy that I killed a man because I had to have him know how come I changed my name, and why I didn't come back through

Vienna, Georgia to pick up my family on my way out west, a half-step ahead of the law.

Not only did that slob we jacks called "Fatman," officially known as "Chief Deputy Edgar A. Floyd," not only did he deserve to die because of the way he bullied people, but I should've killed two bastards for the price of one. I should've killed Sugarfoot too for opening his big mouth. If I'd had a spare minute after turning loose of Fatman Floyd's roly-poly throat in the Green Frog that long ago Saturday evening, I know I would've.

Earlier in the day that Saturday of 1920, that eve of the Fourth, me and Sugarfoot are counting cypress for the super on all-forested, all-wild, hard-to-get-to Bugaboo Island. We're dry for a change, resting in thicket between two Indian mounds that rise up tall as two men. "What did ya hit him with, Bobby?" Sugarfoot asks me. He's referring to a sorry-ass trapper that got conked on the head outside the Expresso Club in Waycross on Friday night. "I know he danced too close to Mildred. And I know how ya feel about them that maims critters in the Okefenokee. So you can tell me, Bobby. Was it a lead pipe?"

We're eating honey I just found—with some biscuits and bacon we brought over.

"A bottle," I tell him.

"A bottle?"

"A whiskey bottle."

"Well I thought for sure it was a pipe or something real hard."

"All ya gotta do is hit him with the rounded edge at the bottom. That way the bottle won't break and you can use it again if the bastard has a buddy, or the bastard don't fall."

I go on and tell Sugarfoot to do his part in crime-prevention by keeping his rambunctious mouth shut. By mid-afternoon, we calculate Bugaboo to be worth at least three million board feet. And we were thankful to get off the game-infested island that summer day without seeing the bear that must've dropped the honey.

"He says he'll be out in a minute."

"Charlie Boy's in the john," I say to Luther.

"Nope. He's on the phone." Luther sets down a cold longneck

Miller and picks up Charlie Boy's empty. He wipes a water ring off the table, then fills my shot glass with whiskey.

"Who's he talking to?" It's me who wants to know.

"Wife, I s'pose. Who else calls? Or gets called from a bar?" Phil, a regular I don't talk to too much, snaps his fingers. Luther goes over to his booth that's also occupied by a new young pretty face. Her stack of frosted hair—I bet it would persevere in a tornado. But pretty. And young. Hell! They're all young to me.

"Deadeye," the scumbag called me. Called me that in front of what could have been some of my friends. That's why Fatman got his balls kicked in, but I killed him because of what he did to the nigger Clarence. "Let me tell ya! I wanna tell ya!" Guess it's in the interest of more whiskey to quiet down.

Me and Sugarfoot are grungy, as grungy as I've ever been. We're grungy because you can't canoe all the way up to Bugaboo. You have to crawl a hundred yards going in and a hundred coming out across trembling earth.

I paddle for a while, then Sugarfoot paddles for a while, then we paddle together again homeward for probably another hour. We work pretty hard at it because, by midsummer in the swamp, the lilies and maidencane leave little open water. Sugarfoot points. Points to a marsh rabbit two feet down swimming like a duck.

We don't need to. Me and Sugarfoot don't need to follow the fish eagles' nests in tall isolated pine trees always several miles apart. And we don't need to depend on hollering, nor inspect the growth on sweetgum trunks, like the old-timers used to do, to find direction in the swamp. We don't need to, because the Herbert Company paid deadman Davis's oldest son good money to set markers in the never-ending prairies and to paint arrows on water oaks in the dark sluice-like lakes. Since all we got to do is paddle, which, like I said, is a pretty mean task in and of itself, since that's all we gotta do, we got time to count gators sticking to just the monsters longer than ten feet. And we got time to gaze at summer wildflowers everywhere that embarrass a rainbow that pops up every now and then. And we got time, lots of time to listen to the differences between the many kinds of frogs.

We come into the homey waters of Billy's Lake and we're

back at the wharf, Billy's Island, happy as blue jays in a fig tree, by five p.m.

Excitement. There was excitement in the air back then in 1920. "GODDAMN EXCITEMENT BATTLED THE PRIMITIVE BAPTIST HEAT." Guess if I don't want the barflies staring at me, I'd better turn the volume down.

Even though most of the four hundred loggers and railbirds won't be in out of the swamp 'til quarter past six, already there's excitement in the air due to it's being Saturday and tomorrow's being the Fourth, a non-paid but day-off holiday. Forty or fifty men, who somehow like us got off early, they're loitering outside the Frog, the general store and the barber shop on Billy Boulevard, the only regularly graded road on the island. What with the flagpole sitter from Macon still up there, I see, the self-appointed crew clowns among the idle men are having an easy time of it.

Can't wait. Can't wait until Charlie Boy returns. Can't wait another second. Yeh—good. Next time I'll tell Luther to just leave the George Dickel, to just leave the bottle.

I grab my hat, the paddles and the canteens. Sugarfoot grabs the company-issued rifles and the survival kits which provide the lost in the swamp with flint, steel wool, a compass and two flares. I tell Sugarfoot I'm going to my pine shanty in the woods to clean up. He tells me he's staying in town. Tells me he has a fresh change of clothes in a locker at the public shower. He hints at one thing, I say something about another, and we go on to decide definitely that we're both taking the seven tram into Waycross again tonight. I tell him I didn't mind that much being with him all day. He tells me to meet him back at Shuford's speakeasy on Alligator Alley for a drink, before going to the Frog to get a bite to eat.

After washin' and scrubbin' at my —HEY—HEY. Miss Frosty has gotten up from Phil's booth and she's walking over to...over to...yep, the cigarette machine. Luther oughta hire her. Put her on the payroll. She could tie a rag to that tail of hers and all she'd need to do is walk across the bar like that again to wipe down all the tables.

Never did.

I never did get all the facts. I had to leave Billy's Island in a big hurry. Had to scamper out of the Frog while Fatman's half-dozen-or-so deputies were under the influence of absolute shock. Though I never did get all the facts, I have had some fifty years to think about them.

My guess is Sugarfoot wanted me in jail so he could have his way with Mildred, a sweet redhead...still sweet, I have no doubt, but she sure ain't still a redhead. I met Mildred when she was working the desk at the Ware County Hotel across Decatur Street from the hotel's biggest customer, Waycross's busy train station. I had come down from Cordele looking for work and I ended up getting a piece of her frothy pie the first day I stepped foot in her hometown. She's the one told me if I wanted to improve my muscles, to check with Mr. MacFarland, foreman with the Herbert Company.

My guess...my guess is Sugarfoot told Clarence, the shoeshiner with a big wooden chairstand outside the barber shop, told Clarence it was me who conked J. D. Connor on the head with a whiskey bottle—then let it be known all over the island that never-harming Clarence knew. I should've. "GODDAMN SHOULD'VE." I should've crammed that worm into the four-foot-wide gator hole we come to, when crawling back to the canoe we left on a hump of hammock in Chase Prairie.

My guess...and I ain't having to guess much since I can't figure any other way it all could've happened...my guess is Fatman didn't know when he got to Billy's Island on the eve of the Fourth, didn't know which culprit he needed to be looking for. He come into the Frog, come in when we was all in there eating and drinking and not praising the lord. Fatman come into the Frog behind six deputies toting hungry shotguns. By the time he made his little speech about the goodness of Waycross society and the danger to it coming from the degeneracy of loggers, by then I knew he knew it was me for sure he wanted. My guess is Fatman wasn't on Billy's Island fifteen minutes that eve of the Fourth of 1920, wasn't there fifteen minutes before he'd heard enough to have had his men rope and drag Clarence down Billy Boulevard about as fast—I have to imagine because all I saw was the bloody, crumpled-up result—about as fast as a horse can go. Sorry scumbag. "THE SORRY SCUMBAG WAS EVEN OUTSIDE HIS FUCKING WARE COUNTY

JURISDICTION." I stare back at the barflies this time because I don't give a goddamn.

Sometimes I wonder.

I wonder if I ever really did strangle Fatman Floyd known around the Expresso Club and several other Waycross dancehalls we jacks were keen on frequenting, known to be a bootlegger and known as the furrier industry's best friend. I guess I wondered it the most that time I went back to the Okefenokee before the awesome fires of '55 and '56, fires that could be smelled all the way down here in Jacksonville, forty miles away. Even before the fires that blackened a hundred thousand acres, even before, the boom town on Billy's Island was gone.

All there was—in 1947 I think it was—all there was, was palmetto in a slash pine forest.

I pulled my canoe up on hard ground out of the murky waters of Billy's Lake. I took my lunch with me to keep it out of the hands of a couple of welcoming raccoons. I went to looking all over the north end of the four-mile-long island. I didn't find a stone from the foundry. I didn't find a rail from the tramway. By the time I didn't find a single board from the Green Frog, nor from the general store, nor from the movie house where we jacks could watch Harold Lloyd hang from real tall buildings any one of three nights a week, by the time of finding just more and more tall pine and short mintgreen palmetto, I had wondered to the point that I favorably considered my innocence.

Should've jumped back right then into the canoe I rented from the government forest people. Should've paddled back to The Pocket and got out of the Okefenokee while my crime seemed like a stale rumor, no more than a long-forgotten little sin. Instead, I followed a game trail toward what my compass said was the island's south end. Birds chirped in some places and they didn't chirp in others. About the time I'd finished dodging one, I'd come upon another seriously-occupied spider web connecting sometimes as many as three and four pine trees. It was the Davis home I was looking for. It was the pioneer family's home I hoped I wouldn't find. The cypress house had many additions. It was shaded in 1920 by the only oaks left uncut on Billy's Island.

Luther pours me another whiskey. He came over on his own this time. I didn't even have to raise my hand. He's good to me. He's the only north Jacksonville bartender I can think of who hasn't—at one time or another—thrown me out. Luther doesn't say anything but I can tell. I can tell from the slant of his head, and I can tell from the way he pours my whiskey that this and all future rounds come with a condition. I'm going to abide. I'm going to be good to him too. I'm going to be better than Sugarfoot. Not only am I letting him take off without my asking for the bottle, but I'm gonna keep my old mouth shut.

Six. Maybe seven. Maybe eight.

When I stopped along Billy's sandy trail to eat my lunch of sweet potatoes and bacon, then several times when I stopped just for resting, I must've heard the cracklings of six or eight deer. Knew it was deer. Knew it wasn't bear, nor no badass piney woods rooter, for I could smell stag musk every time there come up a breeze. Maybe I thought about clapping my hands together like a gunshot, clapping them to see if I could flush one out of the sea of mintgreen. I don't know. I know one thing for sure though. I know I was thinking about that Davis house, how its absence—together with the town of six hundred, together with the town's absence—would make me no doubt a scot-free man.

I should've turned around. Should've backtracked while a mob of butterflies and pine and palmetto was all there was to see. But I was being driven by the want to be innocent. And I was being driven by the walk too, which already had consumed over an hour.

I didn't find the Davis home. I didn't find the metal barrel hoop, nor the iron kitchen stove that the fed forester in uniform at my camp last night, he said might be lying around. I couldn't even find a hole where there had been a well. It didn't matter. Didn't matter though due to the oak trees. It was the oak trees themselves. They kept a smile from crossing my face. When I got into their loftier stretch of the woods, a stretch without a dime of palmetto, the oaks told me undeniably I'd been on the island before. Memories of that ill-fated Saturday in 1920 took charge of me. I walked further south.

"How ya like my haircut, Bobby?"

Me and Sugarfoot are in Shuford's speakeasy having a drink.

There's a bet going on: how long it'll take the stallion hitched outside to break loose and get across Alligator Alley to mount the mare that must be in heat. My money stays in my pocket. I don't like it here. I don't like it because I don't care much for Shuford's fur-trading clientele. Like Donaldson over there. He and a couple of his retards for buddies are drinking homebrewed beer out of a just filled-up pitcher. I'd like to see how much of the beaverskin he's bickering with Shuford about, how much of it I can stuff down his snaggletoothed mouth.

"Got my whiskers trimmed too," Sugarfoot tells me. He pinches his young face. "Even tipped Clarence an extra quarter for the shine he put to my brogans. Come on, Bobby. Speak up. How do I look? Whatcha think about me?"

"I don't," I say. I knock down a slug of Shuford's damn good whiskey.

"You don't?"

"I don't think about ya."

"Damn, Bobby. Ain't no use. Ain't no use trying to be your friend."

Boy oh boy oh boy oh boy. If I had the hammer being sung about on the jukebox which was just fed a quarter or two by Miss Wobbly Butt, by Our Miss Frosty…if I had a hammer I'd swing it in the morning and swing it in the evening too. Boy oh boy oh boy. If I had a simple ballpeen and Sugarfoot was slow enough, I'd fuck up the low-rent bastard's face.

The super. The super's office.

I'd already been to the super's office on Billy Boulevard, me all cleaned up, and the super handed me his personal flask when I turned in the Bugaboo and Honey scouting reports on time. I was up there looking out his window. I was watching the boulevard fill up with more and more getting-off men. I was smoking a factory-rolled cigarette donated by the super, and I took a long slow sip from his flask. I was watching one of the funnier crew clowns imperson-ate the first man to walk on the sun. The crazy idiot hooted like Cheetah, the chimpanzee, and he'd no sooner get one foot down before he'd have it thrown up higher than the other. I was up there looking out the super's window, puffing smoke, when Homer

Danford came running into town.

God almighty I'd like to shout what Homer shouted, but I'm going to be good to my buddy Luther, so I'll just have to whisper: "Model T is acomin' in on the tram line." "So what?" some proud-to-be Neanderthal answered. "I'll tell ya what. It's pullin' a wagonload of fresh women." Homer was right. They were all wanting to celebrate—dressed in red, white and blue. Homer was right. Not only was the wagon full, but a couple of the friskier ones were even riding on the T's high fenders.

Sugarfoot pays for our drinks, his turn. We leave Shuford's—me in a staring match—but lucky for braindead Donaldson and his retarded buddies, we leave without incident. We walk on rutted Alligator Alley past the shoe repair shop that's closed, and we come up on the foundry that's still red glowing inside after six p.m. We're hungry. Mighty hungry. My stomach does somersaults when I see the bulging eyes on the sign out front the—"HOT DIGGETY DOG." Sorry, Luther, but Charlie Boy's coming back. No. Wait a minute. He's stopping off at the bar. His elbows are up on the bar. What the hell's he talking to Luther for?

Sorry, Charlie. Can't wait. Yeh—good. Hope my boy's got the ingrained Townsend foresight to bring the bottle back with him.

The whiteness. The whiteness in the forest.

I didn't even need to see the whiteness in the oak part of the forest that spring or fall day in some year like '47. I saw it, then I didn't see it, due to some tumbleweed. I didn't even need to see the whiteness, the headstones in the pioneer family's cemetery, to know again that I was a killer. I wanted to run but there was only miles and miles of boring pine and palmetto to run to, so I walked up and began browsing dates instead. One stone told me "1842—1899" and told me the bones below belonged to the "King of the Swamp." There were several other dates in and out of the eighteen hundreds that I can't remember exactly, but I do remember there was a woman doctor of sorts said to have cured all, even a couple of Seminoles, and buried alongside her was her pet kingsnake and her three-legged dog. Then—then, then, then—then I come to "1909—1920." It was the Davis boy—eleven years old was all he was—killed, the stone told me, when the scream of the panther in the

Okefenokee was replaced with the scream of the steam locomotive.

"GOLDFISH," I shout. I shout it again in case there's anyone in north Jacksonville not listening, too busy watching Rawhide on TV.

"It was slippery, slimy, bulbous-eyed goldfish," I say to Charlie Boy who is finally sitting back down in front of me. "Sugarfoot is telling much-whiskered Nelson, and whoever else at our table in the Green Frog who'll listen, he's telling us jacks that live goldfish is all the skinny flagpole sitter from Macon will come down for, to eat."

Though it's cool tonight inside and out, in my gut I feel the toothsomeness of the Primitive Baptist heat.

"Personally," I tell my boy, "I'd put on a pound or two since coming in the Frog with Sugarfoot twenty minutes earlier. I'm finishing up enjoying the crispy little tail of the twelfth Minnie's Lake catfish to have blessed my plate, but I'm worried. I'm worried the whole time my brain's gonna get too big from some horse's 'cephalitis."

"Skeeters?"

"Whine after whine. A thousand times more than one."

I hand Charlie Boy his longneck Miller. He drinks it the way I like him to drink it: with reckless abandon.

"Torrence," I say after ridding myself of a pesky fart. "Torrence is the jack sitting at the head of our table. There's a pair of perfect tits from Folkston dressed in blue sitting on his knee. Torrence gets up. She's already gotten up. I saw him whisper something in her terribly obedient ear. 'Hey, Torrence,' I shout because it's so loud inside the Frog that Saturday evening you can't hear the swamp growl, scream and grunt. 'On your way to the privy?' I shout. 'What's it to ya?' he answers back and he can get away with it because he's a big Arkansas boy. 'Just make sure on your way out,' I tell him, 'you bump your scrawny ass with the screen door.' "

"What he say—do?"

"The mammoth was big enough TO SIMPLY CLOSE THE DOOR."

"Pop."

"Yeh?"

"Take it easy."

"Okay."

"Wan sip?"

"Sure."

I love Charlie Boy. I love him because he's not at all like me. I love him too, more and more, because he's such a damn good listener. Sometimes though (like now) I wish he'd get his act confused. I wish he'd barge in and start telling me about his young Jew for a wife or maybe a little something about his overachieving teenage boy. Say anything, Charlie Boy. Say anything—but get me off this beeline of going to tell you that I didn't kill a trapper in a knifefight, I killed a yellow-breasted copper with my bare hands.

Charlie Boy takes his beer back. Doesn't look like he's going to do a damn thing but drink and listen.

"I told you ten years ago, Son. I remember well it was ten years ago. I remember I told you right here at Luther's. I told you I killed a trapper in a fight who pulled a knife that would turn back an elephant, but all I did to him was tap him on the head with a whiskey bottle. I even told you Sugarfoot threw me a lead pipe to hit him with, because I didn't think you'd believe I could kill a man with just a bottle." I look up to find Luther. He's pouring what looks like rum. He doesn't look at me. I'd hoped he would so I could signal with both hands: BRING BEER, BRING GEORGE DICKEL. "I lied, Son, because I didn't want you to know about a slob who some say the scales in Waycross, back there in the teens, wouldn't go high enough to weigh. His name? His name was Chief Deputy Edgar A. (A. for Asshole) Floyd. It wasn't his poundage, Son, that makes me call him a 'slob'. It was the narrowness of his integrity which stood a good chance of being narrower than mine."

"You killed the depty."

"Right. Fatman Floyd."

"Why ya have to kill im, Pop?"

Boy oh boy oh boy oh boy. All these years and finally comes the delicate scare of being at...on the spot. I knew—like I know most things, like I know sextillion follows quintillion, like I know the workings of the internal combustible engine, not to mention what causes the whoosh of the jet airplane; and I know, I know the name of every kind of tree, bird and every kind of ore—I knew— like I know the essentials of most odds and ends—I knew the abundance of alcohol in me and in my boy would work in my favor, would make my job of telling him that much easier. Now if he can just salvage bits and pieces tomorrow, like tonight was a dream. I'll save for another time telling about the bootlegging and the alligator food made of two independent-minded moonshiners. I'll save for another time, while I'm at it, save telling Charlie Boy that Asshole Floyd was lord protector for Junior Blackburn, Waycross's richest furrier. For now—now I'm just going to tell Charlie Boy that Fatman called me "Deadeye" when he asked me what I planned to do about the broken arm and the rib sticking out of the nigger Clarence, the only man on that rinky-dink island I could talk to, talk to for any length of time, without losing my temper.

"Fatman and eight or so of his lackeys were looking for the logger who put a gash in J. D. Connor's head outside the Expresso Club the night before."

"The Ex—"

"A damn nice dance hall in south Waycross where Mildred Shouptrine, a kissing cousin, where she worked. Where? Where was I?"

"Ah...you... you were in the Frog, Pop. Someone walked out."

"Torrence. Torrence and the blue dress walked out. Forget Torrence. Be convinced, Son! I ain't stocking the pond with any red herrings."

Charlie Boy passes me the beer that's nearly empty.

"All thirty of us jacks," I say, "are celebrating, are singing something stupid like 'our country tis of thee' or the national anthem because it's the night before the Fourth, one of the few Herbert Company holidays giving us men a well-deserved day off. We're celebrating and six frigging shotguns storm in the Frog's front door. I look at Sugarfoot. I look at him because earlier in the day I confided in him about the trapper, and I let him be my GODDAMN FRIEND. I look at Sugarfoot because he's the only one I've told that it was me who hit the otter-beaver-coon-bear-fox mutilator in the back of the head as he was getting up on his horse. And when I look, when I look at Sugarfoot, the sorry bastard moves away." I put my fist down with force. "MOVES AWAY FROM ME LIKE A MULLET FROM A SHARK."

"Easy, Pop."

"HEY GODDAMNIT," a barfly I don't know, a barfly in a corner yells at Luther. "CAIN'T SOMEONE QUIET THAT OLD GEEZER DOWN."

I stand up. The bar, the jukebox is silent. I could hear a gnat, if a gnat had to fart. I pick up Charlie Boy's longneck Miller. I don't grab it like a club and I don't bust it. I just sort of ape-study it as if it might prove real soon to be very useful. Still some good beer left and I don't figure this middle-aged squirt to be worth the trouble. I stop studying the bottle. I drink the last swallow. I toss the bottle up in the air, making damn sure to catch it. I cock my head. I aim my left eye. "You'll ease on out of here, fella," I say (even I'm surprised at how civilly I say it), "unless you're not particular about who removes your hemorrhoids."

The weasel, like I figured, the weasel walks out.

Luther waits until the door slams to come over. On his way, he assures the other flies that that dress-rehearsal is all there is for tonight.

"Beaufort Stratton"—I know I'm gonna have to stir shit because Luther usually calls me "Bo"—"you're too old and too good a friend to make me bring you a sermon," and he goes on and delivers a short, correct, probably-needed one anyway. I tell him my boy is on the verge of hearing something he should've heard a long time ago. I tell him, I promise—if he'll bring one more round—his best customer will be relatively mum and out of here rather pronto in less than five minutes.

I'm back. Had to. Had to take a leak. Thought I'd do so while I was already up. Had to rid myself of a pint of rented whiskey. I didn't waste a second in the john. Didn't wash my hands. Didn't even look in the mirror, something I stopped doing decades ago.

While pissing, my ears directed my eyes to a ceiling corner. I watched a spider reinforce the entanglement of a wasp. At first, I thought the wasp had a chance because its wings were buzzing so loud, they were free, and its stinger—poking fruitlessly here and there—was only partly tied down. I knew it was only a matter of time after seeing some of the work of the crafty, net-casting, front legs of the much-smaller spider.

31

Sitting here cross from my good-looking son, I feel like king for the day. "Sixteen tons. What-d-ya get? Another day older and deeper in debt"—must be a favorite of Phil's because he's singing along with...with Jimmy Dean? Frankie Lane? TENNESSEE ERNIE FORD—that's who it is. I take all the credit for sitting here happy as a south Georgia farmer in a light steady summer rain. I take the credit because I've been thinking about gladness since I was spectating while pissing in the john: glad I ventured back to Billy's Island in '47; glad I saw the spider-infested pines and palmetto and particularly the cemetery underneath the oak trees. I'm glad, so glad, glad for the firsthand re-assurance that I once was a killer; glad because I'd hate like hell for my life to have hinged on something that really didn't happen.

Guess I should've taken a bit more time in the john. Guess I should've whacked the fella against the side of the urinal a couple of times. Guess then I wouldn't have a half wet crotch.

"Want more?"

"More?"

"Story."

"Sure."

"Then where was I?" I ask Charlie Boy.

"In the Frog. In the Frog and the law come in."

"Yeh. Not so good. Thanks."

Miss Frosty is staring at me. She looks like she wants me to come over there and strum her optimistic cunt. Sorry, Sweet Thing. I'm too old. I'd have to get to know ya first.

"By the way he moves away from me, Sugarfoot might as well tell Fatman with a bullhorn that I am the one. But it doesn't matter. Doesn't matter a drop because Fatman already knows, I soon learn. The rhino-fathered hippo already knows before he plods through the Frog's front door. I know he knows, already knows, from the spiel he gives after some clown beside him with a shiny badge on too, after some clown gives an introduction with a blast from a shotgun, followed by several blasts on a stupid-ass whistle.

" 'Men,' Fatman says. He tells us he uses the term because there are others, besides loggers, present. 'The dance is over,' he says, and he says it again toying with the words. I'm not gonna try and say it the way he said it, Son, because I don't think you'd care to see your old man throw up. Then he says: 'You. Yeh. And you. Yeh. Don't interrupt. Please, all of you, keep your seats, hear me out. Don't give me a headache. I'm already irritable. One of you muscleheads has caused me to have to eat my fried chicken on the road.' "

"That when you wanna kill im?"

"Hardly."

"Then when?" Charlie Boy asks. He picks up the empty Miller and puts it right back down.

" 'I made the decision for you. I made the decision all by myself,' Fatman tells us jacks and railbirds, and he's telling the waiters and kitchen personnel in the back too, who have put their work on hold. 'I made the decision because of my hunch-turned-conviction that resisting Satan's temptation is too much to ask of...what should I say? what can I say? of breeding rabbits.' I don't think, I don't think a one of us jacks knew what the tub-of-lard was talking about at that early-on moment, but I have to admit we were all much more interested in hearing the sweathog's preposterous insults than we were in arguing with six pointing shotguns."

"What was he talkin' 'bout?"

"Hope I don't have to tell ya in the car."

"How come?"

"Luther's coming...Luther's back."

"Bo, don't shit me now. You in good shape? In good enough control to keep it down?"

"Yes sir."

"Don't shit me now."

"Positive. I wouldn't shit ya, bubba."

"Then you can stay twenty more minutes."

"Twen—"

" 'Til closing time." Luther's hands come from around his back and I think I must be suddenly getting too trustworthy, or simply much too much older. I didn't even notice ahead of time his hands were back there. But God is good after all: a tall Miller for the boy; a rimmer, a full shot, for me.

" 'Last night I was doing my duty as Chief Deputy of Ware County, South Georgia,' Fatman said almost fifty years ago. He said it, Son, somewhat preoccupied with eating catfish pilfered from Dumar and Peter Tom's plates. 'Lest one, or a dozen of you, should want to point out that this here island is half sunk in Charlton County, let me say the law is good, the law's the law, who really cares to be picky when it's only water lilies deciding jurisdiction.' His blue, white-striped shirt is wet with sweat and it's plastered see-through-like to his humongous titties. 'Last night, after my daughter and I ate up an Italian restaurant for her twentieth birthday, I was doing my duty getting a good night's sleep so I'd be fresh on the job this Saturday morning that—woe to one of you—is the week-end of the month I gotta work. I was sleeping soundly when I got a call about an attempted murder downtown at the Expresso Club, too close for comfort to my once-cozy home.' "

"Murrrder?" Charlie Boy asks. He drinks. He asks again after washing down a few of them "r"s.

"Only if I'd laced the trapper's little gash with arsenic," I say, "and I should've. Should've given J. D. more than just a wake-up call. I should've stuck him through with his own knife on account of his inconsiderate, sorry-ass laziness. Sometimes, maybe even often, he didn't check his traps for eight to ten days, to a point when the poor critter's hide was no longer any good." I need to change the subject, but it's so tough when ya feel like you're on a roll. "I'd like to tell you about a rich furrier and his lovely daughter, Son; the furrier, the trapper and ten more trappers not nearly as atrocious as him, the furrier the trappers worked for. He's the benevolent one who I bet made that call, but that's another story I'll save for when we again get drunk."

"Drunk? We drunk, Pop?"

"Passed Sobriety Gorge a mile or two back."

I can't. Goddamn I can't believe it. Miss Frosty is dancing with Phil like she's some kind of tree frog stuck to a pane of glass. All along—shit! —I thought she was pining for me. Gotta concentrate. Gotta tell Charlie Boy all. Gotta keep in mind that good pussy will always be around.

" 'I remember when I was just a pudgy boy, back when Waycross was bigger than Jacksonville,' A-for-Asshole Floyd says. He takes off his Stetson and wafts a tobacco cloud while he looks around. 'Even then I loved being a member. Even then I was at home in the Primitive Baptist church.' His eyes moan. They stop. Stay put on me. 'Most of all I loved dinner on the grounds, next to Jesus, and I doubt any of you syphilitics—particularly you, Deadeye Townsend, particularly you, Satan's best disciplined disciple— I doubt any of you can appreciate the bodacious dishes served up by a wart-free society.' "

"He say that, Pop?"

"That's the best at it, I can remember."

I'd like to toss my shot down, but I think I'm gonna need it more in a minute. " 'When I was just a pudgy boy'—the slob's wearing awful-looking red pants—'back when the train tracks in my Waycross rivalled the number in Savannah, back then I didn't go to school with the son or daughter of a single logger. Now. Now I hear there's a slew of 'em in Kate O'Reilly elementary. Don't. Don't get me wrong.' Fatman's eyes are well-protected. They're surrounded by flesh and deep in their sockets. His eyes move off me. 'It's not the lambs,' he says. 'It's not the innocent children. God knows we'll take care of them. It's the disgusting daddies who come from the dance halls. It's the swamp daddies who want to hang around.' "

"You? You, Pop?"

"Hell no! I picked a sweet-and-sour redhead who knew how not to, who knew better."

"Well."

"WELL WHAT?"

"Don't get off on me. Tell me the thing the depty said that made ya want to kill im."

"It wasn't what he said. But what he said (then him trying to nickname me 'Deadeye'), that made me want to kick him in the balls, which I did, and I got off a clean unmolested punt. It wasn't what he said that made me grab him by the throat when he was down on both knees. It was what he had had his men do to never-harming Clarence who owned the shoestand on Billy Boulevard outside the barber shop, and whom I know for a fact that Sugarfoot told."

"Told?"

"TOLD. Told I conked the trapper on the head with a whiskey

bottle. TOLD. Told while he was getting a spitshine put to his GODDAMN brogans."

"How? How'd ya get close nuf, Pop? How'd ya get near nuf to Fatman, with all them shogguns round, to kick im in the balls? Then time to kill im?"

I raise my shot glass. I only look at it. I don't spill a drop putting it back down.

"The fool offered me forgiveness if I'd only come up and repent; forgiveness, like some preacher-man beckoning on the street. But first—before that, Charlie Boy—first he says: 'Dancing is the root of sexual evil. Don't ask me to burden your reptilian brains with cites from the good book. Just take it from me, a job-secured chief deputy sheriff. Just take it from me, you heard it right here,' he gasps, 'dancing separates the mind from the body.' We jacks, pretty-much entertained so far, we jacks can tell he really believes it. 'Henceforth,' he says. He holds up a catfish skeleton that I stare at, then he tosses it toward the vicinity of me. 'Henceforth, due to Deadeye Townsend's wanton attempt to murder J. D. Connor at the Expresso Club last night,' he gasps, 'not to mention a year of general never-ending logger trouble, HENCEFORTH,' he sallies, 'DANCING IS PROHIBITED IN WAYCROSS, SOUTH GEORGIA.'

"A shotgun blast through the ceiling responds to our standing-up, to our verbal protests. I look around. The jacks and railbirds are all looking at me.

"'Ain't no use,' Fatman says. 'Try Folkston. Try Blackshear. Try Homerville or little Fargo. But ain't no use coming back to my hometown.'"

"Tell me how ya got to im, Pop."

My whiskey goes down the hatch. I put the empty shot glass—in clear sight—near the edge of the table.

"I talked to him."

"What'd ya say?"

"My first thought—truly—my first thought isn't departure in one living piece. My first thought is how much the Waycross dancehalls mean to us sunbaked men—how much they make the insufferable swamp sufferable. But I can tell. I can tell there's no sense debating a maniac. I don't mention the unsuccessful ban on dancing to try and curb voodoo in N'awlins. I don't mention it because I can tell the men's dancehall rights are tied up in the same little bundle with what's going to happen to me."

"What you say?"

"I let my bad eye take a snapshot of him. Then I ask him if choir boys still deal in proof."

"What he say?"

"Didn't say a thing at first. Just stood there moving his head to-and-fro like he's trying to work a catfish bone up or down his throat. Soon he says: 'Even a nigger can be trusted when the truth is all that separates his life from his death.' He motions to one of his lackeys closest to the door. He snaps his fingers. Then the lackey yells at another lackey outside. Then the lackey outside leads a horse through the Frog's front door."

"A horse. Right inside?"

"A horse, Son, with real-bad-hurt but still-breathing Clarence tied across it instead of a saddle. I could see red—rope burns all over his back. I could see a rib sticking out. I could see…could see both arms are tied, but one no longer looks properly attached. Drug him down Billy Boulevard about as fast as the horse could go, I imagine. Never knew for sure. Just knew my plans didn't include sticking around to find out."

"I'm sorry, Pop. I—"

"Know what I did?"

"Ha-uh."

"I have to keep my cool and make Fatman lose his, if I want any chance to get at him, so I tell a short geographical joke. 'Mr. Chief Deputy from Waycross, South Georgia,' I address him. He likes it, I can tell, he's all ears. 'Do you know the faraway African Nile and the nearby St. Johns are the only two rivers in the world that flow north?' He says he knows it, and I'm tickled pink that he does. I ask: 'Do you then also know why them Flor'da crackers in Jacksonville say their very own St. Johns flows north?' The blimp nods his head in the negative like I so much hoped he would. 'Because South Georgia,' I say discouragingly as if having to educate him, 'BECAUSE SOUTH GEORGIA SUCKS.' "

"Good, Pop. Good."

"He stands there, not too far from me, maybe fifteen feet, and his face looks like he's undergoing an attack by his appendix. 'Lord Jesus,' he says, praying toward the holes blasted through the roof, 'give this creature eternal life so I can repeatedly kill him.' He gasps. 'NO. Give him eternal life, forgive him his sins against your Primitive Baptist people,' he gasps, 'if only he'll come to me here in the Green Frog, Billy's Island, and wash my feet.' "

"Never considered it?"

"Not once, Son, in fifty years."

Sometimes I wonder.

I wonder if Sugarfoot really was chuckling as I strolled toward the sweating blob. I wonder: were a washtub and a towel— by a waiter—were they actually brought? Sometimes I wonder. I wonder if Fatman Floyd ever really did put his clammy hand on top my bowed head. Did he really give me an ideal chance to kick him in the balls when he looked around as if expecting applause?

"Well, Charlie Boy, I wasn't about to leave the crowd, leave knowing them shotgun-toters have been instructed by the king of terds to consider my chest to be painted with black concentric circles. So... so I tell Fatman, I tell him: 'Ain't right. Ain't right for repentance to be forced out at gunpoint.' He hears me. I can tell. I can tell 'cause the moon-faced idiot looks at his lackeys like he's thinking about it. 'When you,' I ask, 'when you was back there in Waycross growing up a husky boy, did you? Did you have a choice?'

"Fatman rams his fingers together. Inverting them, he cracks out a short symphony of knuckles. 'Break your guns, Deputies. Break 'em 'til further notice. WE GOT JESUS. Jesus is on our side! He's the only weapon against the Devil.' They do. All do, as if instructed to believe that mob-control calls for obeying each and every order."

"Putty."

"That's right, Charlie Boy. Putty in my hands."

"Pop?"

"Yeh."

"Ready to go?" My boy's holding his breath. Must be trying to get rid of the hiccups.

"Just about. You?"

"Yeh."

"You think—" I point to his empty Miller. I look longingly at my empty shot glass.

"Why not?" my boy says. He's got a smile on his face that would melt what's her name—supposed to be in coming-soon *Cleopatra*. Charlie Boy stands. "Me—I'll get the six-pack to go," he says. "You—you decide where. Where to, Pop?"

"Jake's place. His garage apartment. And Son—"

"Yeh?"

"Beer is good. Beer goes well. Get a pint...half pint of George Dickel."

Sometimes I wonder.

I wonder if I really did smell shit filling up Fatman's red, awful-looking, patriotic pants. And I wonder, I wonder why the jacks and railbirds I'd been so mean to, why when they took control, they were kind enough to let me out. I guess when I wonder these things the most, I always get back to how it could be that Fatman Floyd never had a notion that torturing a nigger might set off a riot. I guess the slob was right. It only got an asshole strangled.

From *A Limited Response*

Barry Handberg

The plane landed at Ton Sun Nut in the early afternoon. After he changed into his jungle issue, Weir's intention was to spend the day and possibly the night in Saigon. Reporting one day late would be no problem and he was certain that this would be his last occasion to visit the city. Last chance or not, after little more than an hour of aimless drifting, Weir gave in to his own lack of energy and caught a ride to the post. As the truck drew nearer to the base he became increasingly aware of his illogical perception that the sooner he got back, the sooner he could get the thing over with.

The driver let him out near the ice cream stand and he walked up the hill to the company. The orderly room was unusually crowded for the late afternoon; but as soon as he entered Stram saw him. The clerk appeared very serious as he broke away from the crowd at his desk and pulled Weir aside.

"I need to talk to you," he said.

"So talk."

Stram looked about the room to indicate that what he had to say was private.

"Let's go outside."

Weir followed Stram outside and around the corner of the building to the edge of the formation area. The clerk's manner had begun to affect him. He hoped there wasn't bad news from the Red Cross.

"Something terrible has happened," Stram said. "Two nights ago, in Saigon, Lt. Joyce was killed. A grenade was tossed into his jeep."

Weir didn't comprehend. Mention of Saigon had just relieved his fear of bad news from home. Joyce's death struck against that rise of feeling and reflected out onto nothing. Weir could only look dumbly at Stram while he waited on the emotional lag.

"Dead?" he was finally able to say.

"Wasted. No one knows for sure what he was doing down there, but they think he must have been seeing a woman. It happened at nine o'clock in a residential area."

"Ohh no."

The half breed. Weir tried to picture her. She came to the depot with her brother-in-law sometimes. Wasn't that what Joyce said? But why had he gone to see her? All that was finished. Weir wiped the sweat from his face and then looked up into hard, bright sky. Dead.

"My AWOL bag," he said. "It's in the orderly room. I need to put it away."

"Yeah, sure," Stram said. The First Sergeant had come out of his office. He was in the process of clearing out the crowd.

"You heard?" he said to Weir.

"I heard."

Weir took the bag to the hootch and tossed it in his locker. After that he walked around to the supply room to pick up his footlocker and his linen. Grunter, who was sorting through stacks of sheets, looked at him intently and decided that he had been informed. "It's a terrible thing," Grunter said.

"You know how it happened?"

"Yes."

"And you don't want to talk about it?"

"No, I don't."

"So how was your trip to Sydney?"

"Good enough."

"And round-eyed women?"

"There were some."

"That's good," Grunter said. "Now maybe you will behave like a true American soldier."

Weir forced a smile and then left. After he carried his gear back to the hootch, he stretched out on his bunk. Immediately he was caught up in a jumbled rush of memories. Women. He recalled the night they had thrown the bottle and wondered if it was love or hate that had led Joyce to Saigon. In spite of the venom that had been

42

in his own heart that night, he hoped Joyce had gone for love. His recent brush with tenderness had left Weir much more open and vulnerable to the suffering of other men.

"Vacation is over; time to go to work."

The First Sergeant was standing in the doorway.

"I just got back," Weir said. "Besides, it's almost five."

"You don't quit being a soldier cause the sun goes down."

Weir followed the First Sergeant over to Joyce's old room. On the way it was explained to him that they needed to inventory the dead man's possessions, so he could clean up the room for the next man. The new CO was transferring from the depot in the morning.

"I don't mind working," Weir said, "but I was wondering if it's all on the up and up, according to regulations that is, for an NCO and an EM to inventory an officer's belongings."

Weir wasn't excited by the morbid possibilities of the task.

"Don't ask me," the First Sergeant said. "I'm just an old man who has been in the Army so long that I've forgotten how to think and can only follow orders. But if it will ease that enormous conscience of yours, Colonel Mitchell and the IG have already looked things over. So have the MPs."

The First Sergeant unlocked the door and they both peered in. The room was in quite a state. Broken glass littered the floor. Joyce's footlocker and both of his wall lockers were open and in disarray. On the desk, the contents of the single drawer were scattered about. The First Sergeant stepped over the glass at the doorway and sat himself down in the room's single chair.

"Sergeant Major said this place was a mess. Damned if he was kidding. The poor bastard must have worked himself up pretty good before he lit out for the city."

"You hadn't seen it before?" Weir asked.

"No."

They began the inventory by sorting out the military issue. Weir collected all of the government's property so that it could be turned in to the supply room. When he saw Joyce's name on the jackets, he was struck by a grim feeling of absolute finality. Joyce had stopped like his father had stopped. Weir forced himself to think of stopping until it scared him. Getting used to a death was the only way to deal with it; there was no way to understand.

"Is his pistol supposed to be here?" he asked.

"No, it was with his body."

Weir spread a sheet on the floor and piled the military goods on top of it, then he tied up the corners of the sheet.

"That's it for the taxpayers," he said. "The rest was his."

The inventory of Joyce's effects began with the stereo system. It took some time. After the First Sergeant had written down the various serial numbers and model numbers, there was some trouble deciding which box and what packing went with each component. When they finally got the system boxed, the First Sergeant called a break and sent Weir for cokes. When he returned there was a full bottle sitting on the table.

"Want a drink?"

Weir looked at the bottle suspiciously.

"Was it his?" he asked.

"Does it matter?"

Weir took a swallow of soda and then poured a small amount of the whiskey into the can.

"Go ahead and take a big one. Ain't no one gonna tell on you. As long as you're drinking with the First Sergeant, you're okay."

Weir twisted on the cap and set the bottle down.

The older man laughed and shook his head.

"Don't make a big deal out of everything," he said. "I don't care if you drink or not. I'm not trying to make myself popular with enlisted men."

"I never thought you were," Weir said.

The First Sergeant laughed again.

"No, I guess you didn't. For a while I suspect you thought I might be trying to have you locked up."

"Weren't you?"

"No, not really. Oh, for a little while, maybe. When I came up the stairs and you were sitting there like a big pigeon, looking the wrong way; I wanted you then, but later it didn't matter. Watching you play slick with Morris was as much fun as putting you in the stockade would have been. Yes, sir, you are very slick with officers. With your style you should have finished ROTC."

"I wasn't popular there either," Weir said.

"I'll bet you weren't."

They finished their drinks and catalogued the rest of Joyce's things. It didn't take long. Outside of the stereo and records, there wasn't that much. Weir folded the two Hong Kong tailored suits and put them in the footlocker along with the single khaki uniform and shoes. The only other garments were three shirts, a pair of swimming trunks, and a jacket made out of a poncho liner. On the back of the jacket a dragon had been embroidered and above the dragon in gold stitching was the motto: "When I die I'm sure to go to heaven, cause I spent my time in Vietnam."

"For an officer and a gentleman, he sure—had piss poor taste."

"I suppose," Weir said.

"You're a talkative bastard, aren't you."

"I always try to remember that free speech isn't guaranteed by the Army."

"Then you damn sure should have done ROTC."

"And end up like him?"

The First Sergeant got up and poured a giant shot into his coke can, then he grabbed the chair, turned it around and sat in it. He grinned savagely at Weir.

"Bullshit. That is pure bullshit and even you don't believe it. That little boy got himself killed because he got the hots for a whore and went busting ass to see her. That is something you would never do, not for a whore or anyone else. If you got blown away, it would be for one of your tight-assed little notions. Who knows what it might be, but for damn sure, it wouldn't be anything so straightforward as pussy."

"Maybe."

"Maybe, hell! You know it's true. Strip away that hippy horseshit and you'll come face to face with one cold, hard son of a bitch."

"Is that why you picked me for this?"

"Shit! I picked you for this cause you were the only one laying on your ass. Everyone else is getting ready for the next high and mighty lord muck-muck to take over."

The remainder of Joyce's effects consisted of toilet articles, trinkets, and a half dozen letters from his parents. Weir was surprised there was nothing from a girl friend or friends in general. He had supposed that Joyce was the type to maintain correspondence.

The First Sergeant wrote up the last items and then, in several trips, Weir transported the former person's belongings to the orderly room. He gave the list to Ray to be typed, signed, and forwarded. It wasn't like slipping Joyce over the side of a ship, but it served the purpose. As Weir was ready to leave the orderly room, the First Sergeant came out of Joyce's old office and spoke to him.

"After you clean the room you can knock off," he said. "But in the morning you're gonna have to start hoppin' on that new jeep. It looks like a pig's ass."

The following morning at work call the company was introduced to its new commanding officer, Cpt. James N. Grant, Quartermaster Corps. The new captain was a man of average height and build who was possessed of that stiff awkwardness that comes to men whose ideals of physical grace have been gained by watching others. In his maiden speech he stressed the importance of efficiency and professionalism in the Modern Army. The company existed for its mission and to the best of his ability he would see that that mission was carried out. Though the Captain had quite a number of other ways to say basically the same thing, Weir hardly listened. Normally he would have, hoping to hear some inadvertent clue to the real man, but now he was just too tired to care. The Captain might be fresh and eager, but he wasn't. Throughout the length of the speech Weir kept repeating to himself: "Get it over with, get it over with."

After the formation ended, Weir was sent to the motor pool to pick up the new jeep; except it wasn't new. The jeep the gleeful mechanics showed him was a rusting, barely running heap. The ARVNs had been given a new heap as part of the effort to upgrade their forces; the jeep Weir was shown was their trade-in.

"Looks like you got yourself one helluva job," a grease monkey said.

"Kiss off," Weir answered.

He spent the next three days in the motor pool working on the jeep and being harassed by the ignorant. In that time he replaced five tires, cleaned the engine, repainted the entire vehicle from sixteen ounce spray cans, stenciled on new markings and got extremely dirty. He also did a lot of waiting while the mechanics performed the higher echelon maintenance. At the end of the third day even the Motor Sergeant was impressed. "It ain't good, but it ain't bad either," he said. The restoration of the jeep was one of the few things Weir had done in the army that he was proud of. Happily he drove it back to the company for the Captain's inspection and approval. The Captain wasn't impressed.

"It looks like a piece of crap," he said. "The first thing in the morning, I want you to take it back to the motor pool and I want you to work on it until it's looking decent. Do you understand?"

"Yes, sir."

Weir did understand. The next morning he drove the jeep to the motor pool and spent the rest of the day hanging around. The mechanics had gotten used to him and were no longer hostile. A few minutes before six he splashed the hose over the jeep to give it a just washed look and then drove it back to the company. On his way to the officer's mess the Captain gave it a quick look and his approval.

"Now that's a lot better," he said.

"Yes, sir."

After waiting another day, Weir went to see Grant and asked to be removed from his position as a driver. It wasn't at all like reporting to Joyce. In front of the desk he saluted and remained at strict attention until the Captain put him at ease.

"To begin with, let me say I certainly don't want to force any man to drive for me," the Captain said after Weir had stated his request. "In fact, if I had the time to pull the maintenance, I wouldn't have a driver. I don't require that sort of gratification."

The Captain's words rubbed Weir like sandpaper. He knew if Grant ever stopped listening to himself and tried to make sense, he wouldn't talk the way he did.

"The question," Grant went on, "is not whether you want to drive, or whether I want a driver, but rather, how is the company's mission best served."

"I thought of that," Weir said. "I have less than a month to go, so I'll be clearing in three weeks anyway, so I thought you might want to pick a new man who was going to be around for a while." The Captain ignored Weir's logic. He stroked his chin in the manner of a professor who had discovered a fundamental error in reasoning, the faulty premise that rendered the argument meaningless. "Has it been the practice in the past to give a man an entire week to clear post?" he asked.

"Yes, sir," Weir said. "But in some outfits they get ten days," he added.

"That seems like a lot of time..."

"It's a big post, sir."

"...especially in a combat zone."

"We don't get that much action."

"I'm aware of that, Specialist," Grant said coldly. "But the men we support, they do get a lot of action."

"Yes, sir."

Weir returned to the motor pool and spent another two days working on the mess truck. On the third day a new driver was chosen and Weir was assigned to Sgt. Hertz to fill sandbags for the new bunkers that were being built. It was a nice change. Each morning after work call Weir and two or three other men loaded onto a duece-and-a-half and drove to a dirt pit that was on the other side of the perimeter near the disposal yard. They usually reached the pit before seven-thirty and they weren't supposed to leave until after five, except when they had a load to deliver. The supply room even provided them with C-rations so they wouldn't waste time driving into the company for lunch. The actual work wasn't hard. The dirt was loose and easy to shovel and they never worked too long at a stretch. Weir was sore for a couple of days, but after being soft and lazy for so long, the sensation was pleasant. For the most part the detail worked without supervision. Sgt. Hertz was the only NCO assigned the bunker project and he spent his time in the company with the other portion of the detail which was doing the actual construction. Hertz didn't trust himself outside of the confines of the company. Presently he was on the wagon and in great fear of this new captain who didn't act as if he would have much sympathy for a poor old sergeant who was near retirement and had

48

a drinking problem. As long as the men at the pit filled enough bags to keep his other crew busy, Hertz didn't care how they did it.

There were also other benefits. Though they were left alone by the company, a small group of whores and young boys visited the sight daily. The boys sold beer and smoke while the whores occasionally performed services in the back of the truck or behind one of the dirt piles. But it was all very low key. They weren't pushy and they seemed content to sit around eating C-rations and chatting when they possibly could have been making the real money someplace else. Weir thought they were refugees from the countryside who were intimidated by Saigon. Whatever the reason, their presence was agreeable. It was nice to have people around who didn't act as if they had been completely corrupted by the war. Weir realized that his values had changed a bit when he began thinking of whores and ten-year-old drug dealers as relatively uncorrupted, but what could he do; just like America, he was growing up.

By the end of his first week on the detail Weir regarded himself as one of the select. The company was going through the change and for those who were around it all day there was nothing but misery and frustration. The clerks and flunkies were caught up in a continuous disruption of inspections, inventories, and reorganizations. No matter how well a job was executed the first time, the Captain was sure to have it done over at least once. This led to a growing discontent among the re-doers. Each evening, after a full day of having done everything wrong, they huddled over their beers and speculated endlessly on when Cpt. Grant would run out of gas. Their previous discussions of art, politics and the relative merits of women fell by the wayside. Like the other peasants they had been reduced to mere survival.

During the early part of Weir's second week of shoveling, Koss was put on the detail. With less than four months until the end of his enlistment, Koss was facing either a medical or a less than honorable discharge. If he went completely nuts and hurt himself, he would get the medical; if his craziness hurt the rules, then he would get the dishonorable. Of course if he held together long enough to get home, the Army wouldn't mind, because then his problems would be civilian problems.

The first day Koss blacked out twice. He was hitting speed and was thin and dehydrated. He didn't seem able to sweat. After his second spell, Weir and the others dragged him into the shade of the truck. They propped him up against a tire and wiped him down with wet T-shirts. When they went back to work one of the whores sat beside him. Eventually he came around and was able to keep look out for officers and MPs.

The blackouts disturbed Weir and filled him with the fear that Koss would die in front of his eyes. After the shooting at Trang's and the death of Joyce, the line between the living and the dead no longer seemed as broad as it once did. Especially now, when Cpt. Grant was seeking to solve his personnel problems as quickly and efficiently as possible. Weir was afraid that Koss would break under the pressure, so in spite of his aversion to renewing their friendship, that night he went to the inventory hootch and spoke with him. Koss seemed to appreciate the conversation but not the advice. Whatever, he continued to hit the speed at his previous rate.

At Weir's first guard mount since his name had been returned to the duty roster, Koss was standing beside him. They had both just shaved and were wearing fresh uniforms. At Weir's insistence they had even devoted fifteen minutes to cleaning their weapons. When he stopped in front of Koss, Cpt. Grant was impressed.

"You're beginning to look like a real soldier," he said.

"Yes, sir," Koss answered.

Cpt. Grant turned to the First Sergeant and explained the phenomenon.

"If you show them how, I think you'll find that most men want to be good soldiers," he said.

The First Sergeant said nothing.

Cpt. Grant pivoted to a halt in front of Weir. He was businesslike again. Snatching the rifle violently from Weir's hands, he examined it minutely. Quickly he found what he was looking for. He thrust the stock toward Weir; his finger pointed at the hinge of the butt plate.

"Do you see that?"

Weir looked down and saw that a number of grains of sand had attached themselves to the grease on the hinge. It seemed reasonable that they should be there, considering that the post was a landscape of bare dirt.

"How long did you spend cleaning this weapon?" the Captain demanded.

"Half an hour."

"Next time you had better reserve an hour of your time."

Grant held out the weapon and Weir grabbed it back. As he thrust it down beside his leg, the Captain whirled away and the First Sergeant came to a halt in front of him. He had a clipboard in his hand and he was smiling maliciously. Weir returned the smile with a who-cares look of his own.

Out of the corner of his eye Grant noticed something.

"First Sergeant, make a note of this," he ordered. "Before Specialist Weir is allowed to begin clearing this post, have him report to me. I want to make sure he has a regulation haircut before he goes home. We wouldn't want the civilians to think we didn't care about the welfare of our troops."

"Will whitewalls be sufficient, *Sir*?" Weir said.

"All I require is a regulation haircut, *Specialist*," Grant replied.

The Captain and the First Sergeant proceeded to the next rank while Weir's rank was put at ease. After the inspection was concluded he took off the flack jacket and flung it into the shade of the arms porch. Fifteen minutes in the sun and the jacket had reduced his fresh uniform to a stinking wilted mess.

"He went after you pretty good," Koss said.

"Let him. He doesn't have many chances left. In twenty-three days I'm going to get on that plane and leave the army behind. Even if they shave my head as I step on board, it'll grow out and be hanging down to my ass before he gets home."

"Right on, brother."

Weir looked at Koss inquisitively and then turned away. It was embarrassing to find out that people liked the crazy bastard better than they liked him.

"I've got a little chicken from the snack bar," he said. "If we end up in the same bunker, you can have some."

"Thanks," Koss said sincerely. Too sincerely for Weir's taste.

As it turned out, Koss didn't eat any of the chicken; he was too busy biting his lips. Right before the mount, he had gone into the latrine and had shot up a whopper kit of speed. He said he did it to protect himself. He knew they wanted to catch him sleeping on guard so they could get rid of him.

"Sure," Weir said.

Regardless of the reason the speed did make him talkative and eager to please. At the bunker he made a great show of stashing his dope like he knew Weir would want him to do. He also told long, humorous, and wandering stories of his family's problems and adventures. The best of the stories concerned the wife of an American officer stationed in Germany, who had tried to buy young Lajos. In a dramatic attempt to alleviate her situation, the childless woman descended upon the refugee camp with cash in hand. The elder Koss, who spoke three languages and had carried his child across the frontier on his shoulders, listened in disbelief and horror to the woman's pidgen proposition. The worst lies of the Russian masters were true.

"I-give-you-money. You-give-me-boy. I-take-boy-to-America," she explained.

"Fuck you," Lajos' father answered. He had picked up the idiom from a friend who had been in contact with American soldiers during the previous war. When the three guards divided the watches, Weir was given the first shift by default. Koss couldn't sleep if he wanted to, and PFC McKissack from the Security Guard Company didn't care. He said he could sleep all day if he wanted to, so it didn't matter to him. Weir thought there was more to it than that. McKissack had recently arrived in the country straight from advanced infantry training at Ft. Polk and was probably lonely. The security company was made up primarily of short-timer grunts who weren't known for their sympathy toward green cherry boys. Even if it was incredibly one sided, conversation with Koss presumably filled a need.

They were all sitting on top of the bunker watching the sun go down when the sector NCO made his rounds. He gave them the password and then sat down and lit up. He said he liked dope as well as anyone, but even so, a man shouldn't smoke late at night when he was awake by himself. By yourself it was too easy to get nervous, careless, or sleepy. They agreed that he was right and reasonable. Weir's watch passed easily. While Koss continued to ramble, he and McKissack listened and ate chicken. Occasionally, they managed to say something for themselves. The atmosphere in the bunker was more like scouts on a camping trip than soldiers on guard. Only once did Weir feel estranged from the general mood. Shortly after the sector NCO left, when they climbed down off the bunker to assume their night positions, Koss clambered around and then stacked his rifle near the exit with the safety off.

"You forgot the safety," Weir said.

"No, I didn't." "It's not on."

"I know that," Koss said.

Weir lifted the rifle from the corner and clicked on the safety. Koss glared at him angrily. Weir didn't know exactly what to do or say, so he leaned the weapon against the wall and went out the exit and down the boardwalk like he was going to take a piss. A few minutes later when Weir returned, Koss didn't mention the incident and neither did he. Gradually the tension dissipated to the extent that at twelve o'clock, when he took off his boots and crawled into the sleeping rack, Weir felt as if he were quitting the party early. In short order, however, he fell asleep.

He wasn't sure how long he slept, but when he awoke Koss was still talking. Weir lay quietly and listened for a bit. Koss was telling lies now, the old stories about the revolutionaries he met in Saigon. And his tone had changed. His voice had energized to a ragged fury. He wasn't loud but he seemed capable of bursting into screams at any moment. Weir twisted about noisily. He hoped this would alert Koss and make him think he was just waking.

"What was that?" Koss hissed.

"It was your buddy rolling in his sleep," McKissack said.

"He's not my buddy."

Weir twisted again and pretended to fall back into sleep. He didn't like himself for leaving McKissack to deal with Koss alone, but he was positive if he got up now, it wouldn't benefit any of them. He had heard poison in Koss's voice when he denied that they were friends. For Koss he was one of *them*.

"Two and a half years of nothing but harassment and now they

53

think they can lock me up."

"You can't do that, " McKissack said. "They put you in Leavenworth forever."

"They'd have to catch me first."

"Where would you go? You'd still be in Vietnam."

"I know places," Koss said. "I've been in jail in Saigon and I know lots of people. Good people. They know I'm against the war. If I killed a few pigs, they'd be glad to help me."

A time went by without anyone speaking. The only sounds that Weir could identify were pacing footsteps and his own pounding heart. He was having difficulty controlling his breathing. The acceleration of his heart was making it nearly impossible for him to breathe through his nose. With his eyes open Weir could make out the silhouettes of Koss and McKissack against the front opening of the bunker. McKissack was sitting at the machine gunner's bench and Koss was standing beside him. Koss had his rifle in his hands. Weir supposed the weapon was ready to fire.

'What was that?"

Weir held his breath.

"What was what?" McKissack whispered.

"Over there," Koss said. "On the road. I saw a light."

"It must be the officer of the guard," McKissack volunteered. "He usually comes around about this time of night."

"They're always sneaking."

Weir rustled and stretched. He was at the edge of his nerve and didn't want to get up, but there seemed to be nothing else to do.

"What's happening," he said. He pushed the mosquito netting aside and climbed off the shelf. His boots were in his hand.

"Your buddy saw a light in the road."

"I told you," Koss warned.

"It's probably the coffee truck. Or has it been by already?" Weir hoped he sounded casual.

"Not yet," McKissack said.

"Then that's what it is."

"Why can't I see it anymore?" Koss demanded.

"They turn off the black outs when they're stopped."

"Sneaking."

"They're not supposed to give away their position."

"Always sneaking."

Koss stepped outside of the bunker to get an unobstructed view of the road. He still couldn't see the truck. To get a better look he climbed on top of the bunker. Standing there he was an easy target for anyone who might be prowling on the other side of the wire. "I still don't see anything," he called down.

"You better get off of there before you get your ass blown away," Weir shouted in a whisper.

Both he and McKissack had picked up their weapons. Weir was scared but not yet ready to shoot. He had to give the man a reasonable chance. Koss could very well be showing off; trying to prove himself with his recklessness. God knows what went on in his burned out skull. If only everyone didn't have a gun. Goddamn guns made everything so absolute.

Koss jumped down on the side of the bunker, putting the structure's bulk between him and the truck he couldn't see. Half-crawling, he scrambled around to the entrance path and up into the bunker.

Weir and McKissack had their rifles ready but not pointed. Koss stood at the doorway across from them.

"Let's go," he said.

"I'm not going anywhere," McKissack said.

"It doesn't make sense," Weir added. "The only thing out there is the coffee truck."

"You're worthless."

Koss started to leave, then turned back. For the first time his rifle was pointed at them.

"If you won't come, you'd better cover me. I'm gonna crawl down by the brim so they won't be able to sneak up on us."

As soon as he was gone McKissack reached for the field phone.

"Don't!" Weir said. "He'll hear you crank it and then he'll think we're in with them."

"Well, I'm not with him."

"Neither am I, but we have to keep cool. When the coffee truck comes I'll walk out like I'm going for coffee and tell them what's happening."

"I have to stay here?" McKissack wanted to know.

"You'll be in the bunker with the machine gun and a rifle."

"Alone."

"Then you go, damnit!"

"No."

"No, what?"

"No, you go," McKissack said.

McKissack moved the machine gun from the front to the side opening, while Weir took a position at the edge of the brim. The waiting for the truck stretched out. Each time he thought he heard a sound, Weir was afraid that Koss had managed to sneak up behind them. At last the truck appeared on the crest of the hill, three bunkers away.

"You going?"

"Not 'till it stops here," Weir said. "We have to act normal."

"You act normal!" McKissack abandoned the machine gun and tried to push past Weir and on out the passageway. Weir blocked and held him.

"Wait! Damn you!"

McKissack shook loose from Weir's grip and went back to the machine gun.

They heard voices and laughter at the truck when it stopped at the neighboring bunker. Weir was fighting the same urge as McKissack. A mad dash to the truck and everything might be over. He fluttered his fingers to relieve a tiny bit of tension.

When the truck actually stopped in front of the bunker he was hesitant to move at first. He was afraid he wouldn't be able to control his legs. The night seemed incredibly bright. As he started down the boardwalk he began to count his steps. He held the rifle along the left side of his body, hoping to conceal it from Koss. Twenty-three, twenty-four.... Suddenly he heard footsteps behind him. He spun around and saw McKissack running toward him. Three shots exploded. McKissack was jerked off his feet and flung to the ground. Weir dove from the boardwalk onto the dirt. Quickly he scrambled along it until he came to a spot where he squeezed underneath. He slid out on the other side and began searching for his target. In front of the bunker Koss was moving toward him.

"Lajos, quit it!" he screamed.

Koss raised his rifle.

"Stop!"

Koss fired and then Weir squeezed off two rounds of his own. "Smoothly," he heard the drill sergeant say at the last moment. After that, his friend was dead.

Roberto de Castro

Ed Marsicano

We sat under a red umbrella on Avenue Atlantica, Rio de Janiero. We drank beer and discussed the price of coffee in Brazil versus the price of coffee in the U.S. The elderly professor smoked cigars. I smoked the local Carltons. The beer tasted good—Brahma. It was three p.m. Clouds hovered in the sky. Girls in tangas sauntered by. We commented on the smallness of the bathing suits. A fat man with a two-day growth of beard sat under the umbrella next to us. The palms swayed as a breeze blew off the Atlantic. A man walked by with a Russian wolfhound tethered to his wrist. The dog stopped, lifted his leg and peed on a tropical plant five feet from where we sat. I told a story of a chihuahua that had urinated on my father's leg at a party twenty-five years ago. They had called my father "Wet Leg" for months afterward.

The squat, unshaved man addressed us. He seemed lonely and looking for someone to drink with. Because we had nothing better to do, I invited him to join us in our indolence. The sun was still hot, but the umbrella shielded us.

We'd been in Rio only a day and a half. He was sixty-two (the elderly professor). I was thirty-seven. We talked of our service in the American Navy—his in WW II, mine during the Vietnam conflict. We decided that most of our military experience had been beneficial.

The squat, bearded man came and sat at our table, under our umbrella. He claimed to be a major in the Brazilian Air Force, although he looked much too fat for this to be true. But we had nothing better to do than to go along with his charade. He seemed joyful, witty, and in need of drinking companions. We had run up a tab, and he ordered more beer. He brought out a couple of 1,000 cruzeiro notes and paid for the new beers as well as taking care of the tab we had run up even before we had met him. His generosity impressed us, and I began to think that maybe this guy really was a major in the Brazilian Air Force. Why would he take the trouble to lie? "I fly the helicopters," he said. But he was so overweight and unshaven.

"I fly the helicopters for twenty-five years. I been in Air Force for twenty-seven years. Today is my birthday."

"How do you say Happy Birthday in Portuguese?" I asked.

"Felice Anniversario," he pronounced the words clearly and slowly. We both repeated them.

We were enjoying ourselves. Rio has that initial appeal. You immediately tend to start plotting your return. The tangas alone are enough to draw you back.

"Que su nome?" I asked in my own linguistic concoction.

"Roberto de Castro. Major Roberto de Castro."

"Major Roberto Fidel Castro?"

"No, Sonofabeech. Roberto de Castro. But do me favor, don't talk about it. I work—no I cannot...I do not... I must not talk now for, you see, a man of my position.... He pointed to a group of drunken American sailors at a table not far from ours. They talked loudly among themselves, and their conversation was liberally punctuated with motherfuckers and assholes.

"I no like American enlisted men. Enlisted men shit. Officers O.K."

"We were both officers."

"I know you O.K. when I see you."

"My father was a policeman," the white-haired professor said, "but he got so he couldn't hear."

"That could be a drawback," I said. Roberto didn't seem to follow the conversation.

"Yesterday I arrive here from Tokyo. Twenty-seven hours on plane. Jesus Christ. Jesus Christ. I am here for one week. I have apartment just behind there." He pointed to a high-rise—one of thousands in the sometimes sunny city of Rio.

"The military give me apartment for when I in Rio." He slapped his right pocket, then his left. "Cruzeiros in this one. Dollars in this one."

He ordered another round of beer and offered me a cigarette. I noticed that his belly lapped way over his belt. He wore shorts, sandals, and a clean T-shirt.

"I learn karate in Tokyo. I have Black Belt." He extended his right hand, his fingers frozen in a ferocious gesture. It looked authentic. I made a muscle to show him. It palled beside his frozen hand. "You macho," he said. "But keep money in shoe. Copacabana very dangerous. Prostitutes have knives. Police refuse to use force. Son-of-a-beeches go free. Jesus Christ. Inflation killing Brazil. Gold in Manaus get mined but Brazil dying. Why? Where does it go? Why Brazil die? Corruption everywhere. What can I do? They pay me and I am happy. Keep your money in shoes, that what I do."

This guy apparently had money stashed all over his body. He came across as a bona fide advocate of law and order. I tended to sympathize with his views of honesty.

We sipped our beer and puddles formed on the metal table. Across the street, on the beach, a young man did perfect pull-ups on an exercise bar. He did twenty pull-ups. His muscles pumped up and glistened in the sun. Roberto de Castro spoke of his next tour of duty. He said he would go to Moscow via Miami, Washington, New York—he had a month layover. His brother, he said, was attached to the Brazilian Embassy in New York. It could be true; his English seemed passable enough.

"How long will you be in Moscow?" I spoke the words slowly so he could comprehend.

"Maybe a year. I don't know. Jesus Christ, I hate Russia. Everywhere I go K.G.B. K.G.B. I say, fuck you K.G.B. They put the bug in my room. I say fuck you all K.G.B. Jesus Christ, Moscow."

"What will you do there?"

"Don't ask me these questions, Sonofabeech." Sonofabeech was my new nickname. But he uttered the words in a friendly way: warmly and with an evident affection for Americans.

A girl in a tanga walked by. She had auburn hair which lay down her long back. She wore a large emerald on her left hand. The three of us watched her intently, our eyes followed the sway of her brown hips. The girl had an uncanny beauty. All of Rio had an uncanny and mysterious tropical beauty. The Atlantic was green and the waves broke close to the shore. Along the shore six hundred yards to the west, in a huge arc, the high-rises faced onto the Atlantic. A city of concrete and glass, from which millions of eyes peered out to sea. The sea from which the Dutch, the Portuguese and the African slaves came. Came to mix and multiply, to fight and enslave one another and to build in the green rain forest. Civilization had come, but underlying the civilized surface lay dark undercurrents. Under the green and white surface were undertows and dangerous eddies.

Roberto de Castro leaned to my right ear. He had beer on his breath, his eyes a bit red. "Tonight I meet two girls from British Caledonia. I meet them in Sao Paulo. They come to my apartment at six."

"Two stewardesses?"

"Si. Yes."

"How old are they?"

"One twenty-seven; the other twenty-two."

"Pretty?"

"Muitabonita. I must go and prepare for them soon."

We envied him in his good fortune. But I wondered how such a fat little man could pick up two beautiful Brits. Then my experience weighed on me and I thought why yes, he is exactly the kind of a man that would appeal to them. He had money, prestige, connections in high places. He probably looked fairly dashing in his uniform, his belly cinched in with a good webbed belt. He was not an unattractive figure. And Walter, the elderly professor, seemed as enthralled with him as I was. Roberto de Castro began to win us over with his conversation and humorous antics. He acted a bit wild but he was proving fun to be with. This fellow had a certain style.

When he excused himself to go to the toilet and to make a phone call, we discussed our faith, with reservations, in his good intentions. We laughed together and drank the beer he'd bought us. The elderly professor was no slouch. With thirty years as a professor of thermal dynamics at Georgia Tech, he was no slouch at all. We had come to Brazil to share ideas and to meet with our counterparts at the Federal University of Pernambuco in Recife. We had done our work and now it was time to unwind in Rio.

The plasterd sailors and marines at the table over from us got up to leave. They took their motherfuckers and assholes with them. We were glad to see them go, for they were getting more blasted by the minute.

"They will be fleeced, the stupid bastards," I said.

"They will be stripped to their drawers," added Walter.

Roberto de Castro returned to the table. He had a big smile on his rugged, stubbly face. It was the face of a seasoned veteran. It was the face of experience.

"The women come here at eight. Margueret and Susan. I meet them here."

"Did you talk to them on the telephone?"

His smile grew wider.

"Pretty soon we must eat," said the elderly professor.

"Where do you want to eat?"

"Let's go for Churiascura."

"You want to go eat with us, Roberto?"

"Nao. When I drink, I drink. When I eat, I eat." His stomach seemed larger than ever. He ordered another round of Chop.

"If I don't get something soon I'm going to be loaded," I said.

"Today, my birthday," he reminded us. We held up our glasses. The three of us clicked them together.

"Cin Cin."

"Salu."

"Felice Aniversario."

A black urchin approached our table. His feet were bare and dirty. He held a bag. His left hand was missing the two middle fingers. He reached into the bag, pulled out two nuts and laid them on the white metal table. Without a word, he was off to tantalize the rest of the cafe-set with his peanuts.

"His bet is you can't eat just one," I said.

"He loses," said the white-haired professor while cleaning his glasses.

Sure enough, in five minutes the little kinky-haired kid was back. He picked up the two untouched peanuts, dropped them in his bag, and held his mutilated hand behind my head—his hand had been permanently altered to form the sign of the cuckold. He stood behind me smiling.

Roberto de Castro and the old professor laughed heartily at this joke being performed on me. I turned around and gave the boy a playful slap on the rump. He giggled off with his bag.

"In Brazil, there are sixteen million little ones who have no houses, no homes. They sleep in the doorways to the big apartment-houses all over Ipanema, Copacabana. Why must this be?" asked Roberto de Castro sadly.

"Corruption everywhere. In Indonesia you put ten dollar bill in your passport. Not under the table, over the table. Corruption in Brazil, corruption in America. Corruption in every country," he added, answering his own question.

The elderly professor nodded in agreement. "Whores of private enterprise that they are," he put in.

"But there is more corruption in some places than in others. That goes for countries and for people," I said.

"The street very dangerous here. I read in paper about a Dutch journalist who get shot just last week. Shot for his wallet. He resist. They shoot him. I ask, where do these guns come from? Why in Brazil do these gangsters have guns?"

"In America everyone has guns," I said. "The gun is a way of life."

"Come to my apartment and I show you article. In 1978, I am in bank. Three gangsters come in bank with guns. They take money. They grab my briefcase from me."

"What kind of guns?" I could hardly believe this.

"38 Smeeth and Wessons. They steal my briefcase, they take my money, so as they leave I have to shoot them. I kill two. The other go away in Volkswagon."

"Did they get the money?" I was having trouble believing what Roberto was saying.

"Yes, I kill one—he put his finger between his eyes. I kill the other one. I shoot him in leg."

"You killed him by shooting him in the leg?" This was too much. "What was your gun?"

"45."

"He bled to death?"

"He bleed to death, police all around and he bleed to death. I had to shoot them. I have no choice but to shoot them.

You come to my apartment; I take shower and change; I show you from newspaper."

"Local hero, eh?"

"Not hero, Sonofabeech. I do my duty as a man of the military. Police no shoot gangsters. If police shoot, there is problem. Why is this? I don't know."

The elderly professor looked at me; we shook our heads in disgust, but we believed every word of Roberto de Castro. Why did we trust this man? It was his style of telling the story; it was his style that gave his story an honest sound. He appeared and acted like a man who had done such a thing. He seemed larger now than before.

By now we were all becoming genuinely endeared to one another. He ordered yet more beer.

"How long you in Rio?"

"Until Thursday. Four days."

"What you must do tomorrow?"

"Not a thing."

"Are you sure?"

"Nothing. Nada. Not anything."

"Tomorrow at ten you meet me at my apartment. We go fly in helicopter, but only for twenty minutes. Can you do this thing?"

"I don't see why not," said the white-haired professor.

"Hell, yes. Where do we fly?"

"Over beach, over Rio. We fly and you look—but only for twenty minutes."

The idea seemed so excellent. A helicopter flight over Rio. I had never been in a helicopter before. The old professor had been in several.

"When I retire from Air Force I fly helicopters from Sao Paulo to Rio. Rio to Sao Paulo. For civilian company. I make good money. Plus I have retirement money from Air Force."

"You should be pretty well off," said the old professor. "They call it doubledipping in the states." Roberto nodded and smiled.

"How much you make as a Major with twenty-seven years in the Air Force?" I asked Roberto.

"Sonofabeech, you ask too many questions. Have respect for your superiors. You have no respect, Sonofabeech."

"Desculpe. I'm sorry."

He smiled again. Then he turned to the old professor and said, looking him right in the eye, "You are like my own father, who is now dead. It is my birthday, I am supposed to be happy and I think of my dead father. He have the white hair like you."
This remark seemed to touch old Walter.
"In Japan, the old ones have great respect. They are consulted on every problem. In America no respect for the old. No respect for the warrior. The soldiers of Vietnam were spitted upon. This I do not like. But it is my birthday and I pay for everything. You are my friends on the day I was born."
Another round of toasts followed.
"We've got to eat, Walter," I said. "I'm getting loaded." Walter was beginning to get a bit tipsey too. Roberto de Castro, however, seemed fairly unaffected by the beer.
"You want especial drink?" he asked. "You try the local especiality?"
"Why don't we take a taxi to this address and eat the Brazilian barbecue?" I showed Roberto a piece of paper with the address of the restaurant.
"I will go with you but I do not eat. When I eat, I eat; when I drink, I drink. Also, I must return here at eight o'clock to meet with women from British Caledonia." He winked at me and rubbed his crotch. "I have party with Scotch and champagne in my apartimiento. Now I look bad, but I will clean myself and change into more better shirts and socks."
I could not help snickering at the rhythm of his broken English, but truly his English sounded much better than my Portuguese.
"Why you laugh, Sonofabeech? Why you laugh at Major Roberto? You have no respect for you elders." Then he stiffened his hand, as he had done before, in the gesture of oriental aggression. "The power flows from the center. Karate is a thing of the mind, the spirit."
I had heard the phrase before. I think it was the title of a book by some Southern writer. I didn't remember his name. He was a good but boozy writer and many people neither remembered his name nor the titles of his books. Too much drinking. Too much to

drink. Too much of everything in America, I thought. Roberto de Castro pulled more cruzeiros from the pocket of his shorts. He laid the money on the table. "Money is nothing to me; it is nothing; it is shit."

The white-haired professor, a tall and distinguished-looking gentleman, rose from the table and offered some of his money in payment. I also reached for my wallet. We had more money than we knew what to do with. Walter had cash for gems—emeralds, amythest, touramelina. He had come prepared to outfit his whole family with gems. These would be his gifts from Rio to his wife and two daughters back in Atlanta. But again Roberto de Castro insisted on catching the tab. He got up and said, "Now we take the taxi to Restorante Leme. You eat sausages, beef, pork, ensalada. All you can eat. We go now, so we be back here by eight. We must be back to meet the women and then I buy the Scotch and the champagne."

Sometimes the whole scene seemed rather confusing, but we were all having such a good time and plenty of money all around. With Americans in Brazil, there is always plenty of money. Brazil is numero uno in world debt. Brazil has an inflation rate of one-hundred and sixty percent. It's right up there with Israel. Brazil, with loads of natural resources, coffee, gems, sugar, seafood, is in danger of going down the tubes. But the American dollar is very strong—a good beer costs forty cents, a good emerald two hundred dollars, a good meal five dollars. And there is also the Mercado Negro. There are underworlds, parallel markets, double standards, multiple identities. Brazil is more corrupt than most tourists can imagine. The police turn the other way. Roberto had been right about everything he said.

The whores carried knives in their purses. The transvestites carried knives in their purses. The Brazilian transvestites were driving the whores from the Bois de Boulogne in Paris. The corruption was being exported.

A Brazilian man of the upper class could kill a mestiso thief, shoot him in the head and leave him to die in the street. He could walk away from this. He did not have to answer, and the policia civila would not make a big thing of it. Such was the state of affairs.

"Before we go I must give you my address, so you can meet

me at ten manana." Roberto took a napkin from the table, borrowed
a pen from Walter and wrote down the address.

"Where is Avenue Gustavo Sampio?" I asked.

"It is just behind this building; it runs alongside Avenue
Atlantica. Here is my apartment number and telephone number.
Where you stay?"

"Hotel Continental—just around the corner," I said.

"This is good; it is only a short walk to Avenue Gustavo
Sampio. You must be there just at ten tomorrow." Then he took
another napkin and repeated the writing of the information. He
handed one napkin to Walter and the other to me. We folded the
napkins and put them in our wallets.

What a stroke of luck, I thought. To run into a man like this
by accident. Normally it would be beyond our means to arrange a
helicopter ride over the fabulous beaches of Rio. This is a thing of good
fortune, I thought. Thank God for fine people like Roberto de Castro.

The final bill paid again by Roberto, we took our leave of the
cafe. By now it was almost six. We had been drinking and talking
for three hours. Directly, Roberto hailed a taxi. The old professor
and I piled in the back. Roberto sat up front with the driver. The cab
sped along Avenue Atlantica, the driver expertly maneuvering in
and out of the traffic. He overtook one car and then the next. The
taxi came to a red light; the driver ran it barely reducing speed.
Another taxi passed us going even faster. A green Mercedes passed
us. There was a woman in the back seat, arranging her hair.

In a few minutes we arrived at the restaurant and the taxi
screeched to a stop. Roberto got out and paid for the trip.

At the door of the restaurant Roberto spoke to the doorman in
an embarrassed way about his attire. He seemed worried about the
inappropriateness of his dress for a man of his position. The
doorman assured him that there would be no problem. Besides, the
big restaurant was practically empty. It was still rather early to be
eating dinner in Rio. In Rio they eat very late and stay out until
dawn. Rio is a city of the night.

The restaurant seemed clean and well-organized. The waiters
wore white shirts with black ties and black coats. We were shown
to our table and were immediately surrounded by them. There was

a waiter for the menus, a waiter for the water, a waiter for the cocktails, a waiter for the white cloth napkins.

In Rio, with the shortage of work, they have to make up little jobs to give the people something to do. This keeps them out of the doorways of the big apartment houses in Ipanema and Copacabana. This keeps them out of the garbage piles on the street. These little jobs give them a reason to exist until they die.

One waiter brought a tray of drinks. Roberto had ordered for us a special round—a mixture of brandy and Campari. We tasted this new drink and agreed that it was a good one—very appropriate for the occasion—the birthday of the Major. Again we toasted his anniversary, as he smiled and raised his glass to ours. The glasses met and clicked, the sound of comraderie in a foreign land.

"Are you growing the beard for Moscow, Major de Castro?" I asked. The Major nodded affirmatively.

"But I cannot talk about Moscow. Do me favor Sonofabeech, don't make reference to my rank. Do me this one favor, eh?"

"Don't worry, it won't happen again," I assured him, and he seemed relieved.

The Major sat back in his chair, putting both hands on his stomach. He sat and watched as a boy brought a long skewer of sausages. With a fork the waiter worked three sausages onto the empty plates before the old professor and me. Roberto refused the sausages. Another waiter brought plates of potato salad, beets, carrots, rice, bread, butter, tomatoes. Soon the entire table was covered with plates of food.

"Eat now," said Roberto, "the food is muito buon." We carved on our sausages as Roberto eyed us, drinking his drink. Another waiter arrived with a skewer of pork wrapped in bacon. Outside in the street I could see the cars of Rio zip by; urchins hawked electric pinwheels that made green arcs in the night; fortune tellers plied their trade; the city of night was coming alive.

"Tomorrow night I have been invited to a dinner for Captain Ralph Blanchard. He is in command of the missile ship that is now in Rio. He is friend of my brother at the Brazilian Embassy in Washington."

My ears perked up. Is he going to take us to a big Naval dinner after our helicopter flight? This man is too generous. This Roberto de Castro is quite a find, quite an in.

"I do not think I will go to this dinner. When I drink, I drink. When I eat, I eat. My birthday is a time for drink."

"How are you going to fly us tomorrow after you've been drinking so much?" The old professor must have been entertaining second thoughts about the whole plan.

"My pilot will fly you, I will only go along. My pilot fly President Reagan when he here last year."

This sounded wrong-headed to me.

"CIA everywhere when Reagan here. CIA in bathrooms. CIA in hotel lobby. CIA in cars and looking out windows. CIA with microphones and guns."

Roberto did seem to know something. His statements would hover on the border of imagination and reality. Still his manner added to his credibility—even if one was not sure; even if there remained an element of mystery. You got the impression you'd never figure it all out.

The drinking, of course, was making the distinctions more difficult to make. Our choices were becoming blurred. Even Walter seemed to be caught up in the flow of events. It was all so new to us. Rio—the sounds of the city, blaring horns, laughter from unknown mouths, strange whistles from dark entrances, tiny tangas, exotic bodies, big jewels, fast cars, unspeakable filth, rats in garbage, the stars over the Atlantic, guns in coats, knives in purses, CIA, KGB, helicopters, Moscow, Rio, New York—all of this flew by my mind; it twirled and twisted like the electric pinwheels we had seen on the street. Carnival never stopped; it went on forever.

Young British airline hostesses. You could look on page ten of the *Latin American Daily Post* and see: Alone in Rio? Have the best time of your life. Contact the most sophisticated worldwide escort service. Transform your dreams into reality. Indulge yourself with pleasure, leisure, satisfaction in the company of beauties. Take home good memories of our young and attractive escorts who will transform your private world of contentment—the English was always a little bit out of whack. The whole scene seemed about one bubble off level.

The old professor knew better, so did I. We were not snotnoses lost in a haunted house. We were old veterans like Roberto de Castro. We could turn down an invitation. We knew better; and yet we were carried along by the flow of events, our spirits fueled with beer and brandy and sausages and the Major's grand ways.

He looked like a drunken, cussing old sergeant on a tear, but he acted like a major. He spoke pretty good English; occasionally he dropped phrases in Japanese and French. He flew around the world; he had helicopters at his disposal. He knew the captains of warships, diplomats.

He had an apartment at a fashionable address.

A waiter brought a skewer of very rare beef. It looked unappetizingly red.

I took only one small piece. Roberto de Castro had not touched one morsel of the elaborate meal set before us. I could tell that the old professor was getting tired.

We finished dinner; we could eat no more, and still plenty of food lay on the table. Roberto instructed the waiters to remove the half-empty plates. He ordered them with the authority of one who is used to calling the shots. A man in control of every situation, any situation.

The waiter brought the check, handing it to Roberto, but the white-haired professor took it from his hand insisting that we pay for our own meal. I reached for my wallet with similar intentions. Roberto regarded our actions. We handed him 10,000 cruzeiros, which maybe amounted to ten dollars. He grabbed the money, balling up the paper notes in his hairy fist. He had the hands of a Hyde, not a Jekyll. Then he tossed the money onto the marble table top.

"I pay, not you."

We insisted.

Again he picked up the bills, balling them tighter this time. He tossed the ball of paper money on the table.

"This is nothing to me; money is shit. Jesus Christ, money is nada." But he did not reach in his pocket, as he had done at the cafe.

"We will pay," I said, unfolding the ball of money. Then

71

Roberto acquiesced, resigning himself to the fact: "OK, if you want to pay, it doesn't matter to me," he said.

We paid the waiter and stood up to leave. We had only about thirty minutes to get back to the outdoor cafe where the airline stewardesses were to meet de Castro for his party.

"We will walk; it is not far," Roberto said. Then we found ourselves back on the cut-stone pavement of Avenue Atlantica. The bars and restaurants were all open now, and the street was alive with people. A towering female impersonator bared her breasts to Walter. Then a black hooker beckoned us from the corner, waving, smiling, twitching her butt and saying "Anything you want." I tried to not pay attention. Waiters at every cafe enjoined us to sit and drink, to have something to eat. Taxis and buses drove by, expelling their noxious fumes into the cool night air. We could see the islands off shore, dark humps in the moonlight.

A man in a crowd screamed in French that someone had stolen his watch. But no police were around and no one paid him much attention.

Roberto said, "You must be careful here in Copacabana; you must watch your wallets, watches, jewelry. There are many thieves."

One could not belabor the point enough. Rio is the pickpocket capital of the world. They cut your pants with a razor, the wallet silently drops into their hand. You feel nothing.

We walked along briskly; the old professor sweating now and beginning to pant. Roberto in the lead. I looked at my watch; it was almost eight. Would we miss our meeting? Would the party be over before it started?

At five minutes to eight we got back where it all began—the cafe near the Hotel Continental in Leme. We sat at a different table. Roberto immediately signalled a waiter and ordered three beers.

"They have told me on the phone that they are coming here around eight tonight. Then we go to my apartment and I take shower and put on my good clothes. But first"—he was speaking rapidly now—"I must buy the Scotch and the champagne. There is store for this right around the corner."

He stood up without finishing his beer. And he had not left an unfinished beer all day. The man drank like two fish. He reached into the pockets of his shorts.

"You give me money for the Scotch and champagne, I will give it back. I pay you back at my apartment. It is no big deal."

I pulled my wallet, extracted two 5,000 cruzeiro notes, and handed them over. Walter, who was still panting from the fast walk, handed him two more, and Roberto said, "One more is all we need for the good Scotch: you want the best for the birthday and for Susan and Michele." Walter passed him a third 5,000 cruzeiro note.

And then Roberto was off around the corner.

It took about thirty seconds. Maybe a minute. I looked over at Walter, who slowly sipped his glass of beer. I opened my wallet and removed the napkin with Roberto de Castro's address and telephone number written on it.

"Walter, let me see the napkin he gave you." I compared the two telephone numbers. Of course they were different. They did not agree. They were out of whack. We were out of whack.

"I don't think we will see the little fat bastard again," I said. He had only been gone for a minute and we both knew.

"But he paid for almost all the beer and the taxi; we had to practically fight him to pay for our own dinner," I said, arguing with myself.

Walter, the old engineer, had already computed our loss.

"He never shelled out more than 5,000 cruzeiros. Beers are only forty cents. I figure he got us for about twenty-three dollars which will keep him in alcohol for a week or two."

I started to laugh. The old professor laughed with me. Were we mad? Could we be very upset? Shit, we had more money than we knew what to do with.

"It was a good show. He was clever—the son of a bitch."

"It's not the money, just the principle of the thing."

"Delusions of grandeur—all of those grandiose plans— helicopters, parties, apartments on the beach—he was just another two-bit con man."

"We played it pretty stupid, and the alcohol didn't help."

"Let's just keep it between ourselves. No sense in making ourselves look bad," said Walter. "You know it's terrifying to get everything you want. That's what puts people in these messes to begin with."

Roberto's beer still sat there on the table. I lifted it and poured it into my glass.

Lord Short Shoe Wants the Monkey

Bob Shacochis

There's a jazz club in Barbados that you end up in after hours. You come in hot from the streets, fight your way to the bar for an ice-cold Banks beer, and take it easy taking it all in. Tonight there's a big deal going down. Lord Short Shoe wants the monkey. He says he's willing to pay.

The tropical night is kinetic and full of potential. In a place like Bridgetown, there's something going on somewhere, and it won't be right—you'd be stealing from yourself—unless you're there, too. So you come in from the streets, a damp ocean breeze coaxing you through the wrought-iron gate that leads up the stairs to the second story of this run-down Victorian relic, its pink gingerbread crumbling with termites. You are already sort of perfectly oriented—the fact is, you feel great. On the streets the people were good-looking, carefully dressed, friendly. There's no rampant poverty here to close you up or make you defensive. You have witnessed the subliminal movement of moon from sea, the silhouettes of palm trees and sailboats framed in its orange hoop. Dinner at the Frangipani was excellent, the superlative cuisine of this island: flying fish, baked christophene, an arsenal of curries, blood pudding. You drank a rum punch that turned out to be a solvent for every piece of trouble and bad luck you ever experienced. The conversation at the table was full of adventure and brotherhood and, between the men and women, love was ripe and sticky and abundant—enough for all. You felt so much a part of it, and to be a part of it all is what you've always wanted.

So you push through the crowd at the door, into an atmosphere of latent sex and laughing words and jazz, past the drunks and the heroes, past the world-class drifters and lean sailors, the silent dealers, the civil servants, and the deadly men with politics in their heads, the sunburned tourists and the beautiful Bajan women who flare their dark eyes at you as you rub past them and say, *"Here now, watch yourself, boy. You think you cahn handle a brown skin gy-url?"* At the bar you wait several minutes for your bottle of Banks to be snapped down in front of you by a lanky bartender who's got on Ray-Bans and an undersized T-shirt with the logo *Survival Tour '79.* It's not like the rum shops on the side streets and alleys; there's paint on the walls, no one pays attention to you, and the clientele seems safely cosmopolitan.

The jazz is sweet enough to keep a dying man alive until the set is over. Sitting in at a table next to the musicians, there's a stunning black woman singing a soft scat that explores the melody just below the acoustical level of the instruments. You think you recognize her and you're right, you do. The lady is Melandra Goodnight, backup vocal for the calypsonian from Antigua, Lord Short Shoe. The group performed earlier tonight at the cricket stadium. Melandra's still dressed in the white sequined gown she wears onstage, a piece of sartorial luminescence in front of the spotlights, string straps supporting coconut breasts that spark like the flashbulbs of paparazzi, the skirt slit on both sides to the top of her hipbones. What a sight Melandra is onstage when she spreads out her glowing black legs and the front and back flaps of her gown swing down between them like a long, elegant loincloth, her hips marking the beat while she grips the microphone with both hands and sings, sings with every muscle of her body. If you're a woman you respond to her with awe and envy. If you're a man, the sight of Melandra cripples you with lust.

Eyes closed in concentration, her head bobbing, she's floating in the music and you stare at her freely, wondering if you should move closer, be bold enough to sit at her table, buy her another Coca-Cola, which she seems to be drinking. At least she has one hand wrapped around a half-empty bottle of it, the long, red-tipped fingers encircling the glass. The inevitable image rises in your brain and you can't get rid of it, can't stop imagining that hand on you, so you turn away to watch the musicians. There are seven of them, seven old black men, five parked on wooden chairs arranged in a semicircle in the shadowy corner, the sixth on one side caressing the keys of an ancient upright, the seventh dusting the traps on the opposite side, behind Melandra, all of them unmindful of the audience, unmindful of the years by the dozens on the road spreading the gospel of jazz to houses that loved the message but not always the messengers. They have come here, like you, to take it easy, to do what they want. Luckie Percentie, the octogenarian on the alto sax, a New Orleans man with a lot of wind left. Shake Keane, the man who conquered Europe with his trumpet. After twenty-odd years he's come home to the islands. The Professor on clarinet. Few people in the States know he's still alive. Little Dalmar Gibson on the big baritone sax. It was Mezz Mezzrow who showed him how to blow the beast, in Harlem back in the thirties. Dulceman Collins hasn't been back to East St. Louis since he was a teenager, but they still call him Poison Ivory there and talk about him like he never left. Rubin Hopper, the dark-skinned Krupa, and Les Harvey, the guitarist, both Chicago-born and bred on the blues. There's no way you can put your finger on what they're doing. One ear hears a tangle of roots, the other a hedge of flowering hibiscus, and Melandra's voice dipping from bloom to bloom like a hummingbird.

You stand there taking it all in, drinking two or three fresh Banks, brewed down the street. More and more your attention returns to Melandra. You begin to throb; it starts in your heart and works its way down. Your hand shakes somewhat as you light a cigarette. She's moaning now, following the saxophone up into the hills, into the bush. The air is suddenly wet and dripping and all you smell is her sex. A monkey screams nearby. Something somewhere is howling. People turn to look at you. *My God!* You reel down the length of the bar to get outside on the balcony.

On the narrow balcony that hangs over Front Street, Harter and Short Shoe are squeezed around a tiny café table. Several bottles of Guinness between them, the white man passive and serious, the black man passive and serious, trying to come to terms. The monkey is there, too, behaving itself, eating coco plums and a wedge of papaya. Both men look up briefly at the guy who comes staggering out from inside the club, knocking into chairs, his eyes glassy, his crisp chinos stretched by a terrific hard-on. A coke head, thinks Harter. He looks back at Short Shoe, who nods with insincere pity.

"Dere's anuddah white mahn come too close to Melandra," Short Shoe says. Harter, irritated by the calypso singer's sly, mocking tone, sighs and flicks his cigarette down into the empty street.

"What's wrong, bruddah?" Short Shoe says. "You cahnt take a joke?"

Harter insists he doesn't want to sell the monkey, says he loves it, but talks like he has a price even though his one proposition so far was said in jest, at least that's what Short Shoe figured, and Short Shoe wants the monkey, wants it to put in his act to promote his recent hit, "Dis Country Need a Monkey":

We need a monkey
To govern dis country
Take any monkey
From any monkey tree
Give him a big car
Ahnd a pretty secretaree
Den dis little monkey
Make a big monkey
Outta we.

There are four more verses, each progressively broadening the insult against the island's prime minister.

When the record aired on Radio Antilles last month, the fellows at Government House in Antigua sat down to discuss the pros and cons of grabbing Short Shoe and giving him a lesson in lyric writing. He got the word that the bigshots were visibly unhappy with him, knew it was only temporary but decided it was time to take the band out to the islands, work down the chain to Trinidad, and then maybe a couple of dates in Georgetown before taking the show north to Brooklyn and Toronto. He was airborne in a yellow Liat Avro before the bookings were confirmed. The performances they did were sellouts, sneak-ins, crowd crazy. The record shops in each place couldn't keep the forty-five stocked.

But Short Shoe knows that something is missing in the repertoire. He has a fondness for props and gimmicks and drama, anything that will make him stand out and contribute to his growing legend. Wearing shoes with the toes cut out of them was a decision of this nature. They symbolize, he says, his boyhood and his humble background, his ties with the people. When his momma couldn't afford anything but trouble, her son inherited charity shoes from the Bosom of Love First Baptist Church. No size seemed to fit his awkward feet, so he chopped off the toes of the pair that appealed to him—dusty black wingtips—with his machete. He wore them for eight years. Now he wears Adidas with his meaty toes poking out the front. He will not tolerate any humor about big feet. The shoes, he says repeatedly, are a symbol, not a joke.

Melandra first joined the group with the debut of "Coffee Grinder." During the chorus Short Shoe would leap up against her and grind away from behind. With the song "Leggo Tourist Lady," he became more ambitious. On the beach, he found a plump white girl down vacationing from the States. Prepared to pay, in one way or another, for her services, he was still not at all surprised when she immediately agreed to accommodate him in any way she could. He waited for carnival and the calypso-king competition. He waited until the end of the set to do the song. As he began the second verse, she pranced out onstage from the wings and took his arm, put her pink cheek against his chest. "Leggo lady," he sang and shook her off. She persisted, hugging him around the waist. "Leggo tourist lady," he sang breathlessly, and danced away from her. She fell to her knees and crawled after him, wrapping her arms around his shins, trying to pull him down. "Leggo tourist leggo." The crowd on the parade grounds took up the chant. The percussionists banged down into it with brake drums and congas, unleashing total bacchanal, a frenzied, drunken spree. Short Shoe sank lower and lower onto the white girl until almost on top of her. Then the horns drilled back into the beat and Melandra, undaunted Melandra, pulled Short Shoe up by his ear and kicked him in the ass. He finished the song in triumph.

The King.

He realizes that he has a reputation to uphold, that he must give the people all he can, and in return they will love him and allow him the wealth they themselves will never have. There's a vision he's had since he first picked out the notes of the monkey tune on the old Buck Owens guitar, red-white-and blue paneled, he keeps next to his bed. He sees himself as he knows his fans must see him under the lights: clean and big and randy, his beard the right stroke of revolution, a savior in extrasnug white bell-bottoms, or at least a prophet, the voice of his people, a bull, a rogue angel, a star.

He sees himself onstage. The shrill brass salutes Melandra's entrance with the monkey. They dress the little fucker in an executive blue shirt jac and schoolboy shorts. The word *Boss* is screened on the back of the monkey's shirt in red letters. Melandra straps a toy holster and pistol around the primate's waist. The monkey dances around in a circle, does back flips, pretends to shoot at the crowd with the gun. At the end of the song the monkey hops onto Short Shoe, climbs him like a tree and balancing on top of Short Shoe's ropey head, pulls down its tiny shorts and moons the audience. Glorious. This is what Short Shoe pictures in his mind, but so far he hasn't been able to re-create it for the world.

The first time they tried to use a monkey was in St. Kitts. The monkey bolted offstage as soon as Melandra let go of it, never to be seen again. In Montserrat, Short Shoe made his next attempt, asking around if anybody had a domesticated monkey for sale. Nobody had one on hand, but as soon as the news spread that Short Shoe wanted a monkey, every ragged kid on the island went up into the mountains to find him one. Out of the many brought down from the bush, he chose the one that seemed the calmest. He purchased a light chain at the hardware store; some ganja-soothed Rastafarian in a leather shop took an entire day making the monkey a little collar. The calypsonian introduced the monkey into the act three nights later. Short Shoe clipped his end of the leash around his wrist so his hands would be unencumbered while he danced and sang. When Melandra tried to put the clothes on the monkey, the monkey sprang onto Short Shoe's thigh, viciously biting him over and over. The music stopped, the band members rushed to help. The monkey drew blood from all of them before they could unfasten the leash from Short Shoe's wrist. But the dream still lives for Short Shoe. It is a good idea, and good ideas make money. He knows he can make it work if he only finds the right monkey. As always, the knowledge

that he must give the people what they want drives him onward.
Indeed, before he even reached Barbados two days ago the word had been passed through the grapevine that Short Shoe was looking for a monkey. Anybody who gave any thought to the problem arrived at the same solution: *Hahtah got himself a good monkey.* And that's what they told Short Shoe when he landed.

"So what about it," Harter says. "You like this jazz stuff?"

"Yeah, nice," Short Shoe answers quickly, peering around like his attention should be elsewhere. He's tired of bullshitting, which is a very new feeling for him, but all he can think about is getting the monkey. They've gone through five rounds of Guinness and gotten nowhere. Harter has been tonelessly monologuing diesel engines and Hollywood. The monkey looks bored, rolling a papaya seed under his hairy forefinger around the wet tabletop. Short Shoe decides it's good strategy to call for a bottle of Mount Gay.

Nobody knows much about Harter, but everybody claims to know him, and everybody has a different version of who the slim, aloof, sandy-haired Californian living in quiet luxury out on Bathsheba Beach is, and what he's doing on the island. He's going to build a hotel, he's filming feature-length pornography, he runs a safe house for Bolivian smugglers, he's a retired pirate, he's involved in some baroque deal with the government, a casino or banking scam, he's a Hollywood star who decided to dump it all, he's CIA investigating that Cuban plane somebody blew out of the air awhile ago. Nobody knows, but everybody's sure it's something big, because in his quietness, in his stylish solitude, in his tense but confident movements, Harter appears to be a man of importance.

The waiter brings the bottle of gold rum, two clean glasses, a small bucket of melting ice. Short Shoe pours a full load for both of them. As politely as a Boy Scout, the monkey reaches into the bucket, fishes around, and takes one small piece of ice to suck. He watches Harter expectantly, letting out little chirps every once in a while, birdlike and questioning.

"My monkey here has a lot of talent," Harter says assertively. "You couldn't ask for a better monkey."

For lack of much else to do, Harter has been training the monkey for the last six months. Somebody out at Bathsheba shot its mother for a stew, found the terrified baby clinging to a dead teat underneath her protective arms. Harter heard about it and on impulse went to see the hunter. The mother's skin, pink and fly-covered, was stretched and nailed to dry on the door of the man's shanty. Not knowing exactly what to do with the baby, the hunter placed it inside one of the many empty oil drums in his dirt yard for safekeeping until the proper time came for him to study the situation. Harter stared down into the darkness and saw the honey-sheened, cat-sized ball of baby monkey hiding its face, trembling in the absurd immensity of the drum. He paid fifty cents for the three-month-old vervet. He named him Frank. They had had some good times together.

"Dese monkey too much like politician," Short Shoe says, now readily suspicious of both breeds. "How I know dis monkey trustable?"

"Because I said he is, pal." Harter is trying to work himself up to the deal.

"Take it easy, mahn." Short Shoe explains what it is he wants the monkey to do in the act. Harter, another State Express stuck in his mouth, stands up and slaps the surface of the table.

"Come here, Frank," he says. The monkey scurries out of his chair onto the table, stops erect in the center of it at the point Harter has indicated. Like a gymnastics coach, Harter works through a dry run of a black flip with the monkey, picking him up and turning him in the air and setting him back down. He does it three times, finally rewarding Frank with a coco plum from a canvas bag next to his chair.

"Okay, Frank," Harter says, taking a step back from the table. He snaps his fingers and the monkey executes a precise back flip, landing in a half-crouch right in place, the bottle and glasses undisturbed. "Again," Harter commands, snapping his fingers. Frank does it again. Harter takes another step away from the table. "To me, Frank, to me," Harter says. The monkey back flips off the table, onto Harter's shoulder, and is given a coco plum. Frank squeezes the fruit as if it were a lump of clay.

"Hey," yells Short Shoe, jumping up from the table. "Hey," he yells to nobody in particular. "You see daht? My God, mahn, dis a smaht monkey. I must have dis fella."

"Sit down and let's talk about it," Harter says. All three of them, black, white, and monkey, take their former seats. Harter doesn't want to sell the monkey, but he does have something else in mind, something that lodged there like a wild bullet the first night Short Shoe brought the band to the island and Harter went to catch the show. There's an urge gnawing away at him, growing out of control. He makes his proposition, the same one he joked about before.

"Holy Christ," Short Shoe says, withdrawing, but he's already puzzling over the diplomacy he will have to use to make it happen.

The success of their negotiation can be measured by the bottle. Two-thirds full and they're both still insisting the other wants too much. At the halfway mark, Harter is assuring himself that Short Shoe will come across, and the calypsonian realizes he will, after all, leave the place with the monkey. The details just have to be fleshed out. With only a shot left for each of them in the bottle, the deal is struck, and they toast each other. Short Shoe will take the monkey on tour for six weeks and then return him to Barbados. Harter will take Melandra for a night. The monkey has fallen asleep, curled up on the seat of his chair.

Was there coke, too, a little snow to clear the muggy air? You can't remember. Nor can you remember the woman you were with earlier in the evening, nor why you left her and came here to the jazz club. Lately life has seemed so fragmented, a blurred series of wonderful postcards, of clever vignettes. There are so many excuses available: the dizzying tropic sun, the high-octane rum, the lethargy of many days at sea, the casual violence of West Indian streets, the wrenching juxtaposition of an expensive sports car racing through the ghetto. Yet you have resisted the slow disintegration of moral certitude that is a part of it all, right? The unexpected blow to your senses that plunged your brain down between your legs was nothing more than a normal reaction to an exotic woman, and what you imagine is not lurid, sweaty sexual acrobatics but a seaside cottage, Melandra singing for you alone, toffee-colored babies playing in the sand, a milk goat in the yard, a parrot in the lemon tree. Sounds nice.

Leaning on the balcony for the last half-hour, trying to calm

yourself, to regain the cool you walked in with, you have eaves-
dropped on their conversation. And now, you think, it is your
responsibility to speak. Possessively, protectively, you approach
the table where the imposing black man and the humorless expatri-
ate face each other. With obvious satisfaction, they are polishing off
the last of their bottle of Mount Gay. You stand there unsteadily but
with righteous fortitude until they glance up. Maybe Harter figures
you want to pet the monkey. Short Shoe guesses you are a fan of his,
that you will congratulate him, ask for an autograph. You clear your
throat, which wakes the monkey.

"Gentlemen, forgive me," you say. "You cannot trade a
woman for a monkey." It sounds so right, so absolute. You are
pleased with yourself.

"Where dis fella come from?" Short Shoe cries. You recoil
from the threat in his voice. "People buttin around like dey own de
fuckin world. Mind you own business, Jimbo."

"Get lost," Harter adds, scowling at you.

You suddenly feel fatuous, and a little hurt. You escape to the bar.

Short Shoe wanders back in, the monkey clinging to his side,
and sits down next to Melandra. Her hair has become less sculp-
tured in the humid air, the silver eyeshadow blotchy and creased,
her lip gloss flat. She is dying to get back to her room at the Holiday
Inn, slip off her dress and high heels, take a shower and collapse into bed.

"Let's go, Shorty," she says. "I am tired."

"Rushin, rushin, ahlways rushin," Short Shoe says. "Gy-url,
I believe you mus be commun*ist*." Instead of laughing, she cuts her
eyes at him. "Look here," he continues, "I get de monkey."

"I see it."

His mood changes abruptly. Melandra's enthusiasm, he thinks,
should match his own. Leaning over the table, he strokes the
monkey and looks straight at the woman with what he hopes is the
right amount of regret.

"Darlin, l get meself in a terrible jam wit dis white fella," he
says with great seriousness." Be nice to him ahnd he say he forget
de whole thing."

Melandra's eyes narrow as if she's taking aim on Short Shoe.

She feels on the edge of a temper but pushes it back. Her voice is her pride and her living: to let anger race through it would be like dropping a cooking pepper into hibiscus honey.

"How you mean, Shorty," she asks, her silky voice just the slightest bit strained, "'be nice'?"

The monkey fidgets in his big hands as he pets it harder. Short Shoe knows he was lucky to find such an exceptional monkey, luckier still not to pay cash. The woman is not going to ice such a sweet deal, even if Short Shoe has to hold her down himself.

"Doan play de fool wit me, womahn," he says, shaking a finger in her face. She looks at it, a mongoose watching a snake. Then she sighs wearily and turns away.

"Do ahs I say."

"No."

"He want more dahn just a night, ya know. I tell him no. I thinkin in your best in-*trest*."

"No."

Short Shoe's voice rises an octave. "How you mean, 'no'?" he shouts, and smacks the table loudly with his palm. "I tellin you *yes*. You forgettin a lot ah things, darlin. How many womahn in de world want to sing with Short Shoe? Ahnswer me daht." Short Shoe is proud of the fact that he always takes an international view of his affairs.

"Shorty, doan do dis to me."

There is such a look of disappointment on her face that Short Shoe is momentarily confused—actually on the brink of catastrophe, because he is *never* unsure of himself. But the people in the bar begin to applaud the jazz musicians, who have just finished their set. Short Shoe multiplies the applause thousands and thousands of times and throws it all down on himself, letting it swell his chest with glorification. His is the voice of the people, he must give them what they want.

"Go now, I tellin you," he orders her. "Go!"

She smooths her hair back over her ears and then fans herself with a paper napkin. Melandra realizes that whatever magic Short Shoe performs onstage, however great he truly is in front of an audience, he can still be a clod at the dinner table, a half-literate fisherman. She likes him enough so that working with him isn't a hardship, she is grateful that it was her he chose to sing with him, because that changed her life in a way she never believed could really happen, but Short Shoe is like most men she has ever met—selfish and single-minded. Men were all just schoolboys in uniforms diddling with their little peckers.

She pictures herself out in the countryside at her momma's house back in Antigua. She and Momma are in the kitchen, talking about all the troubles and woe *men does give dem*. Melandra opens the cupboard and takes out the tin can Momma keeps full with hibiscus honey. She takes it out to the garden, to the pepper bush, covered with the small green cooking peppers that must be taken out of the stew before they burst and make the food too hot to eat. *One cookin peppah, two cookin peppah, tree cookin peppah*—into the honey. She takes the can back inside and puts it on the kerosene stove. *Momma, I goin to boil dis up ahnd give it to de next mahn try to make a fool of me*. Momma looks at her and shakes her head sadly. *Gy-url, you does de boilin ahll you life den*.

"Ahlright, Shorty," she says in a deadly voice. "But dis monkey goin come bahck to haunt you, ya know." She sneers, sucks her teeth in disgust, and walks away. On the way out to the balcony she brushes up against Shake Keane, the trumpet player, and whispers in his ear, "Bruddah mahn, check me out in a while, hmm? I goin outside fah some action."

"Yeah, baby," Shake says. "What's up?"

"Showtime," Melandra answers wickedly.

There's been too much rum. Harter really doesn't know what he's doing but he knows there's more than just a rum spell on him, that he has a powerful yearning for a black woman, that he heard their skin is always, permanently, as hot as the Tunisian desert, and it sends a fever running right through you, that some white men can't stand the heat, their blood pressure or something can't take it, but for those that can, heaven is a step closer. And he knows that Melandra is one of the most majestic women he has ever seen, and that these moments with her might knock him out of the drift he's been in for the past year.

Harter watches Melandra approach his table. She stays in

focus and everything else gets blurred. His head hangs loosely but his eyes are geared up and he watches her, watches her perfect hips dance through the mostly empty chairs and tables, the long graceful dark arms shining, her huge chestnut eyes, her thin nose that suggests some East Indian blood, lips as full as pillows, straight shoulder-length hair that he recalls puffed up in a big Afro on Short Shoe's last album cover. She has taken a pink hibiscus flower from one of the tables and placed it behind her left ear. Harter can feel his pulse struggling up through the alcohol.

"Please sit down," he says in what he thinks of as his Hollywood voice. Charming and jaded. "You are beautiful. Absolutely."

"You such a polite mahn," Melandra answers coyly. Harter hears the staged quality in her voice but he's too far gone to infer anything from it. "Shorty say you lookin fah me. True?" She pulls a chair next to his and sits down, crossing her legs so that the skirt of her dress falls away, exposing one leg fully up to her hip, the other almost so, and the elastic fringe of a black G-string. Harter tries to keep his attention from this area, knowing that he must produce some facsimile of romance and sensitivity if this is all going to work right.

Melandra's surprised that he's as handsome as he is, and as drunk. She expected some pasty bastard, dressed like an off-duty cop, a good decade older than Harter, sober enough still to enjoy the nasty little routines that men buy women for. She thinks maybe she might be interested in Harter under different circumstances. His eyes aren't totally cold like she imagined, but green and cautious and lonely. Maybe she can talk him out of this foolishness, let him buy her dinner tomorrow night; Short Shoe can keep his monkey, and she can go home to bed.

Harter unfreezes, reaches over and grabs her arm, not painfully, but hard enough to annoy her. Her first instinct is to slap him. She stops herself—it's too easy, it might well do more damage to her than put anybody in their place. Harter and Short Shoe would shrug it off, absolved, and she did not want that, she did not want to defer to stalemate or forgiveness. Not this time. Not against a monkey. It's clear that the only way out of it is her way.

"I—love—you," Harter says, as though he has searched long

and hard for each word.

"Is daht right?"

"Uh-huh."

"Well, love mus have its way," she says, throwing her arms around his neck, tugging him forward, smothering his mouth with hers, her tongue driving, she hopes, far enough down his throat to choke him. Harter's bewildered resistance lasts about two seconds. He never knew he had it in him, that *any* man had it in him, but he feels as if he's about to swoon. Melandra is running her fingers through his hair, raking his scalp mercilessly with her sharp fingernails. His lips are being pulped by her forceful kisses. His eyes are closed and feel like they are never going to open up again, as though there's some electrical glue being pumped into him. It all feels so natural, so deep, so meant to be. He's lost in what he believes is the sudden inevitability of their passion, lost to the world, sailing on some mythological ghost ship with the Queen of Africa. He slips a hand under the top of her dress and clutches one of her breasts. It *is* hot. Her nipple feels like a pencil eraser.

Melandra's hand glides from Harter's shoulder to the top of his shirt. She pops all of the buttons in one aggressive rip, peeling his shirt back so she can rub and knead his bare chest. A groan hums in the back of Harter's throat. There's some thought, some urgent information, trying to form in his head but he can't make it clear. *Baby*, he gasps, but then his mouth is locked up again by Melandra's. Her hand crabs its way down his tan stomach. Before it registers with him, his belt is unbuckled, his fly unzipped. Her hand snakes into his linen pants and grabs him. The vague feeling he's been trying to define spears through the darkness like a spotlight. *Not here*, he shrieks to himself. The light dims, the power fails. This is Harter's last coherent thought of the evening.

Melandra cocks her head slightly, steals a look out of the corner of her eye at the faces gathering around her. They affect her the same as any audience does: A part of her performs for them, a part of her sits back and observes it all ambivalently. She's as good an actress as she is a singer, lets her imagination accept whatever role is required of her—Shorty's stupid on-stage games have at least given her that. Her hand works deftly, conscientiously; she hopes the rings on her fingers aren't bruising the man too terribly. She imagines she's rubbing ointment on a baby's arm, or milking Momma's cow, which is easier because of the noise Harter is making. She suppresses the desire to fall out of her chair laughing; Short Shoe's foul covenant has the right-of-way here. Harter begins to arch his hips off the chair. Melandra stops, but too late, for the spasm has begun. She wonders if she should feel sorry for him for what she's about to do. It's a curious thought, and maybe some other time she'll allow herself to explore it. But right now she imagines the cooking peppers bursting one by one.

You are sulking, having one last Banks before you call it a night and head back to where you're staying. Most of the jazz musicians have sidled up to the bar around you. Short Shoe's there with them, showing off the monkey. You'd like to talk to them but you can't think of anything appropriate to say, something to let them know you're not just another drunk tourist hanging on the bar. The trumpet player strolls in from outside, a generous grin on his face, and announces loudly, "Look here, check this scene out on the balcony."

Everybody moves out from the bar and you follow them. Before you can even get outside, Short Shoe is already pushing his way back in, a grim, uninvolved expression on his face, muttering *Dread, dread.* He hurries for the exit, wearing the skinny string-bean monkey like a necktie.

There's hardly room for you on the small balcony. Beyond the weak illumination provided by a single, bug-swarmed light bulb above the doorway, the night is at its darkest point. You squeeze through the crowd, excusing yourself, begging the pardon of those you perhaps shove more than you should. You break into the front line. The sight of Melandra fondling Harter before your astonished eyes turns your heart upside down.

"Mmm hmm, lookit that gal bone the chicken," one of the gray-haired musicians next to you drawls. "Gawd*damn*, that looks good."

Harter might as well be knocked out. His head lolls over the back of his chair, his arms and legs sprawl out to the sides. Melandra has moved away from him just enough so the audience can witness this most flagrant of hand jobs, delivered under the auspices of Melandra's professional devastating smile. As Harter begins to ejaculate, the spectators clap and hoot. Harter reacts to the noise as if it were cold water. His head snaps straight, his eyes click open wide with horror. You watch the stain on his pants spreading and think, oh yes, this is a fine specimen of sin and shame in front of you. Harter stares dumbly down at his lap, at the dark relentless hand that still grips him. He tries to wriggle backward, to get the hell out of there, but Melandra has him tight.

"Fellas," she calls out triumphantly, "look aht dis little vahnilla bean." She waves Harter's prick at them, which can't seem to lose its erection. "Looks like it might be ready fah busy-*ness*, if de boy evah grow up."

She wags him stiffly at one or two faces. "Somebody got a nice disease dey cahn give dis mahn? Something to help him remembah dis ro-*mahnce*?" Harter struggles up. Melandra plants her free hand on his chest and shoves him back down.

"Monkey," she hisses, pointing at Harter. "Womahn," she says, jerking a thumb at herself. She repeats the distinction: *Monkey. Womahn.* "Lissen to me, fella. Monkey ahnd womahn doan mix. It seem you make a big mistake. Now get you ahss away." She releases him and steps back, her arms folded over her breasts, glaring at Harter, threatening him with every last ounce of trouble she can.

You shudder, regaining your senses, tasting the bitter-sweetness of such severe and utter humiliation. But you have to hand it to Harter. He doesn't panic. He composes himself quickly and with, you must admit, a certain amount of dignity. Slowly he puts himself back together, beginning with sunglasses which he takes from his shirt pocket. He lights a cigarette. Only then does he straighten out his torn shirt, and only after his shirt is right does he return himself to the sanctuary of his linens and zip up. When he is finished, he stands solemnly in front of the gathering, exhaling the smoke from his State Express. You suspect he is going to speak, but he only shrugs, offering a half-smile that concedes the evening to Melandra. Then, with athletic sureness, he vaults over the railing of the balcony to the street below and is gone.

Months later, in a bar in Mustique or Negril or maybe St. Lucia, you hear the end of the story. Someone who knows will tell you that in Port of Spain, at Short Shoe's first performance at the Boomba Club, the Calypsonian was attacked by a man in a gorilla suit who proceeded to beat him with a stick. And Melandra, the fellow at the bar will say, has signed a solo contract with Mango Records. They even gave her her own backup band to tour with. She has a new single that's just been released.

"Maybe you've heard it already on the Voice of the Antilles," the guy says. "It's called 'Troff de Monkey.' " Sure, you tell the guy, waiting for the foam to settle in your beer. You've heard it. Throw off the monkey.

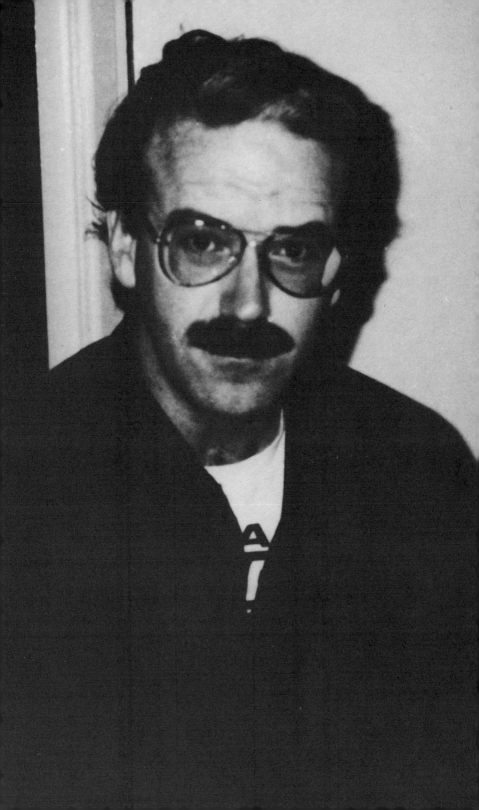

from *The Square Root of Fun*

Gary Scott White

Never believe fate's more than the condensation of childhood; how often you overtook the beloved, panting, breathing hard from the blissful chase after nothing, but into the open.

                                        R.M. Rilke, The Seventh Elegy

∘ *Litany* ∘

The door was not reluctant. A creech recorded a certain amount of friction between jamb and base when the air suddenly became a breeze. It obeyed according to its devices, or lack thereof. It was white and not well painted. Frozen waves rippled down it, not pronounced, but evident enough. The toe, the toe attached to a slim bony foot that dangled in the air near the door, did not react. It maintained a sway that bordered on stillness and appeared to be oblivious to what the creech meant. If she'd been asked if she'd been tapping her toe in the air she'd certainly have denied it. And why ask? It would only disturb she who was so easily disturbed. He could not think of a good enough reason, though he was curious because she'd never dangled her bare foot so before and he thought it might depict some inner sense of gaiety, her barely noticeable tapping. Or perhaps it was poetry she was reading now. She's noticed the suggestion of movement in the door's white paint and it reminded her of mud flats. Her remembrance then added the white to the flats which changed the place where they might have been because sun-bleached mud flats are not found in many places. Where were they found? She wouldn't want to ask such a question in such a situation. He might take her seriously.

The breeze found its way around the corner of the building and in the open window beside which he sat propped up against the

95

wall. He wasn't wearing a shirt because the heat was terrific. The bed under him wore only a crumpled cover sheet and a fitted sheet the first of which stretched half the length of the bed in shadowy mountainous relief. The door blew shut but not loudly. The breeze closed it gently as if it had the dexterity to do so again.

His left foot was pulled toward him, its heel in close proximity to his right hamstring and its toes tucked beneath the shadowy mountainous sheet. The billowing pale green curtains hid him from view when the breeze came into them. Then they parted and fell back as if unswallowing the air they'd gulped. He still had his eyes closed but she wondered if he'd opened them when he was obscured. She turned a page in the book held before her by her left hand with her right hand and looked above the first sentence on the top of the page uncovered on the left to supplant her curiosity. He let the lids of his eyes drift apart, exposing their hazy sky blue pigment held in place by a pinkish white circular field that diminished inward and focused on her loose sanguine figure with its hovering book-hand attachment. Canned laughter seeped through the wall she was slouched toward. He turned his head a little to the left, in the direction of this sudden occurrence of sound as if there might be something of it to see. She did not react, remained stolid of mien, almost stern. Her dangling foot, bare and slightly blackened on the bottom, twitched nevertheless in accordance with the tickling movements of a comic fly. His thoughts were invisible to her and hers to him but his were more obviously so. His eyes had closed now but his head had not returned to its position of rest. Nevertheless, the wall behind his eyes appeared to be holding them up.

The comic fly, having been twitched away, clownishly circumscribed its own path with a buzzing that varied in loudness, the reason for which neither could ascertain, he with his ears only, her with her ears and the peripheral attention of her type tracing eyes. The buzzing stopped. Quite suddenly, simultaneous with the end of the comic fly's noisy progress, the shaft of sunshine that had been pouring through the yard gap between the pale green curtains, which now hung still, vanished. Its adorning parallelogram was gone, leaving behind an expansive dull plane of flowery-print infested lino. The fly, esconce the F key of the dusty typewriter, jumped into the air but the key did not budge. The physics were wrong. Neither noticed this but she did note the new expanse and he, eyes still lightly closed, sensed a slight drop in temperature. His body welcomed the sensation and encouraged his thoughts to approve. He almost smiled faintly in accordance with these just demands. The hanging panels of enfolded pale green linen were puffing up and so threatening to come between their faces again. They had had nothing between their faces for longer than it takes a breeze to end since the funeral. The fly, apparently bored with entertaining them, left, it must be assumed, via the window. Neither saw it go. When he opened his eyes they were looking down. As his gaze steadied, it observed the interfaces availing themselves to his sight range: the roll of tummy flesh against the soft blue cotton of his loose draw string pants, the same soft blue cotton against the crisper, tighter white cotton of the cover sheet, the shadowy underfold of the same crisp white cover sheet against its exposed fold crests. He did this abstractly, looking for more than was there. The sunshine spread itself once more across the flat flowers in the lino. The sunshine reclaimed its prescribed section of floor with the calm, even motion with which a wand is waved before a rabbit is lifted by its ears from a hat. She'd stopped on the word "harbinger," had plucked it from its place of interdependence and was moving it around in her head, savouring it, sucking on it, prodding it, looking for more in it than was there. He raised his eyes and with them the plane of his face. Their rovering focus finds a crack in the wall opposite, which runs from the angle it makes with the ceiling down to the upper part of the arm that holds the book aloft before her. "Harbinger" is losing its grip on her. She consigns it to the lexicon from which it came before appearing on the page in front of her. The crack, if a stream, as he imagined, would need to be the result of patient water on a fairly level plane because it was more straight than curved. At least it had no gaps, no breaks to hinder his imagination. Thin subsidiary faults in the plaster suggested themselves as tributaries. Toward her end it began to delta. He had to squint to see how literally her blurry shape functioned as a gulf for this crack system. She felt his squint and turned a page even though she'd not finished reading the one in front of her. Dialogue reared its head, was nudging its way forward into a more concrete form, beyond the acknowledgement of presence. If she reproved him, his retort was ready. "What an oddly realistic crack system." Oblique enough but not too studied an observation meaning, "Oh, did I disturb you, sorry, I was just looking at the crack on the wall behind you." She'd read most of the books in the box, one after the other, without skipping around by choice, just randomly grabbing another, working her way to the bottom of the box through the layered flat ones and the intrusive ones standing on their ends to fill in the gaps made necessary by incongruent dimensions. He did not intend to mention his observations concerning her amorphous gulfdom, which only appeared when he squinted at the crack discoursing along the wall behind her, unless she spoke first, or looked up at him, or feigned irritation in some notable way. He did not intend to begin an exchange of words between them. A truck passed loudly on the street outside the open window. The area of floor claimed by sunshine blinked as if it had a lid because the basement aspect of the room caused the body of the truck to pass between the window and late afternoon position of the sun. She'd collected the books from her mother's flat. There were a few in every room but a shelf full near the television in the sitting room. She'd taken nothing else. The noise of the passing truck punctuated dialogue's bid to become more concrete with a dash '—', a parenthetic pause to separate distinct portions of presence. This particular book found it difficult to hold her attention but she'd struggled through many of the others in the box, too, and had taught herself to continue, to persevere. Clues were not plentiful, or were very cleverly disguised. The flowers lit up by the rectangle of sunshine in the middle of the floor seemed more alive than those that remained in the sub-street level shadow which softened the light in the rest of the room. They seemed a bright bouquet by contrast despite the wear of diverse footwear on the feet of diverse renters over the years and the occasional scuff mark on the tangled petals and stems. She was tiring, her eyes were turning against her. He let his imagination go, its roving egged on by an itch inside his head that he couldn't reach, that he couldn't just close his eyes and scratch away. He let it, his anxious gaze, drift down to the bouquet that seemed now, to him, to be standing, detached from the plane of the linoleum, up. He began trying to identify the types of blossoms represented in the weirdly vivid bouquet. He wondered should he seek assistance. Her eyes completely refused to focus and, in league with her powers of concentration, overthrew the polity of her intention. The result was a mild form of physical panic which disallows the body stillness. She moved her head, both arms, and began to tap her air-bound toe in earnest, all in a bit of a fit, suddenly, at once. There was a rose, definitely, and a carnation, and an iris, but what were the little blue ones, of which there were several? What were they? Under the table — which had a number of things on it besides the dusty typewriter — leaning against the wall was a picture, obviously a paper reproduction of a painting, framed, and covered with glass. She absolutely had to move. They'd slept facing one another to keep the other's presence constant. They'd slept lightly in each other's wake as if each could feel the lid action of the other's eye physically, but without touching them. A wine bottle, empty, and therefore a dim transparent green, stood by a disgorged loaf of bread and some sweaty cheese. The cheese had a brownish rind very nearly the same colour as her tawny, rush bristled, skin. He felt her agitation and took his chance. He spoke. The reproduction was of an interior. A woman stood before a dressing table balancing a hand held scale. Her face was an exquisite balance itself between rigorous concentration and solitary whimsy. He knew the painter immediately. The subject and use of light were unmistakable. His voice drew her face around toward it with gravity, as an unseen operatic voice heard while walking in narrow streets might, pregnant with a sense of wonder, even beauty. "I've been having the same dream. I had it again just now. It's fairly simple and very clear. When I wake I think it happened, just for a moment, each time. I've had it five or six times since the funeral, yet your mother isn't in it. Perhaps my subconscious doesn't know her well enough, can't conjure her up."

His voice moved into the captive quiet of the hot air like the fingers of a masseuse poignantly seek muscular tension. It became aware of its own sound and judging that it might be allowed to continue, without interruption, began to answer itself, became rhythmic, melodic, began to sing. Her eyes did not seek out those of the speaker but became ears. They looked ahead and down a bit but saw nothing in particular, did not focus. A white pitcher with blue markings roughly based on the shape of a leafy plant had a big ear which, no doubt, was also listening to his sonorous monologue, as were the wall and all the characters and personages portrayed and encased in the cardboard box which was open and had floppy ears of its own.

"I'm walking very briskly along a gray wet street through a dilapidated part of a city that seems accustomed to being gray and wet. My brisk step is causing the toes of my shoes to flip dirty water off the pavement up over themselves and up as far as the cuffs of my trousers. I am delighted by this and walk and flip all the more briskly until I come across a door which I push open with some grace as one can with a door one knows well. If my toes had been bare, and fingers, a snappy beat would no doubt have announced me." Her toe, through his reference to toes, tapped in the air consciously now and, though this at first confuses it slightly, causing it to lapse into an embarrassed rounder action, it soon gains the confidence it requires to tap willfully in the air and takes off in earnest. This new tapping quickly becomes a partner to the resonant dream being spoken into the room and a certain amount of interplay materializes between them. It is difficult to say how much control she has over this harmony but her nerves have definitely gleaned a soothing bounty from his dulcet tone.

"A bell tinkles spritely as I clear the door. It sounds surprised. The cafe is deserted. Languid. As surprised as its bell to encounter such pace. An olive-skinned waiter, a boy still, perhaps the son of the proprietor, eventually appears from the rear of the cafe. His eyes ask me what I want rather than what I'd like but he is silent. He is wearing a T-shirt with the image of a Grecian urn on it depicting a winged god in mythic context." The hanging folds of linen dyed the colour of young limes were puffing their cheeks and blowing balmy air into the room. They also threatened to come between their faces again but as his voice continued unabated and contained his presence he was possibly more unsettled than she by this chance of brief divorce. He is watching her hear him in an effort to animate his talking which he fears might wear on her patience if it begins to drone.

"I look more closely at the image but I am unable to determine its context because the young face above it is so severe and impatient for my order and also because the T-shirt itself has been washed many times and the epic representation is faded. I ask for tea and a roll while my right hand slips into the inside pocket of my jacket to assure itself that the envelope is still there. The contents of the roll, strangely, varies. Last time it was cheese, the time before that sausage, the time before, last week, egg mayonnaise. I can't help thinking, now, having noticed this, that my subconscious is mocking me, is trying to lure me into believing I can choose the filling in the rolls of my dreams, that I'm free to choose the filling, but that choosing the filling is the full extent of my freedom and even that choice will remain illusory, unless recognized as mockery. I am waiting for my father who, it now becomes clear, I am to meet in the cafe."

She has closed her eyes now and is allowing her head to swim with the heard words as they resound into the quiet of their enclosure. He notices this and looks at the floor. The rectangle of sunlight has stretched like pulled taffy across the scuffed floral design embedded in the linoleum flooring, distorting the side furthest away from the window, its source, just to the left of his shoulder, into a blunt wedge which is pointing towards the cardboard box which is sitting beside the chair in which she is sprawled, toe tapping in mid-air. His eyes begin retreating, told by his mind to stop dragging them back into focus when all visual powers were required in the memory banks, the mind offering its speculative aside as evidence of this defection. He does not, therefore, notice that soon after closing her eyes she also grinned perceptibly. He continues to speak.

"The bell startles me. I have lost the spring I entered the cafe with. I'm chewing as he scurries into the chair opposite me across the table. I notice I'm tasting nothing. He is very agitated. His hair is as wild and tangled as his gaze. He is speaking urgently to me as if instructing me in some sort of plan. I cannot understand him. He is not using words. Or at least not words I know. My right hand reaches into the inside pocket of my jacket and it is still there. He becomes terrified by my movement and grabs my right arm to keep any subsequent gesture in check. I am confused and don't know why he is begging me in gestures and sounds I cannot identify as words. Then he scurries off in terror. I am numb with confusion. I pull the envelope out and look at it knowing no more about it than ever. The severe boy waiter appears suddenly, kisses me on the forehead and takes a sip of my tea. My eyes are fixed on his faded T-shirt when I wake but I cannot fix its context."

There was a lag of reverberation between the last syllable he spoke and the ensuing silence which coaxed her attention toward pleasure. Her thoughts raced to substantiate the experience and were aided by the replete nature of the quiet in the enclosure caused by the complete feeling of coming to an end the recounting of his recurring daydream took. He did not expect comment, so when he noticed the broad grin spilling from beneath her closed eyes, he felt relieved and amused. His eyes, now allowed full range of focus power, found the picture leaning dismounted against the wall, the dismounting of which had inspired her only spoken words since the funeral. "Do you mind?" The hanging panels of pale green puffed up every minute or so, threatening to come between their faces.

Sunshine streamed in beneath them when they billowed illuminating more scuffs on the floral linoleum.

◦ *Prone* ◦

A game of insomnia. Suddenly he heard clapping. It came from somewhere up the street possibly the square, but suddenly, not prompted by music or any other sound. The applause was not thunderous or sharp nor listless and obligatory. It participated, as now he tried to participate in it, though with little success. Each time her breathing and his thoughts removed him from its context before it came again. Each round drone of this overheard collusion between praise and participation therefore surprised him and caused him to wonder at it anew. Perhaps a hundred claps, two hundred hands — it was a low, even sound. A juggler? A troupe of clowns? No voices aside, from passing talk, no voices were, or seemed to be, causing these swelling and diminishing intrusions of human night noise. Each time her breathing, even and close, enveloped and relieved him of inexorable curiosity about the source of these capricious bouts of smothered uproar. The three: a. she—her close, even breathing, no, snoring; b. the distant applause—its humanity and caprices and c. the dark—that cloaked but salubrious envoy; conspired with the pleasure he felt for such conspiracies to elongate his wakefulness by making of it a game of tag based on a hide and seek mode. When the curtains billowed he watched the skin on their pale underbellies unravel and hold, for as long as it takes a breeze to end, their breath. She was asleep, face dimly lit, body flat out, and grazed by just enough light to suggest skin. The dusty typewriter, which they'd found dumped in an alley near their room and which was missing many letters—two vowels and eight consonants—but possessed all its numbers and punctuational capabilities, was shining. It caught the direct illumination offered for safety by a street light which was attached to a building, another hotel, across the street. This light came across their bed at an angle of approximately fifty five degrees, an angle proscribed by the position of the window in relation to the bulb at the centre of the glow. This shaft of light, which shot between the gray panel of curtain nearest the bed and the window frame, did not move across the room as did its counterpart during the day. It was static, excepting its gradual slow appearance and disappearance, its angle and area of possible illumination. The three played tag with him, but not their sum, which was based on his sleeplessness. Her light snoring was pacific: it lapped; he was sprawled on its beach.

Again, the controlled intrusion of engaged clapping, a round drone, the base tone static of a remote untune-in-able station complimented by the veiled attitude the night has toward the senses. She was asleep, at last, book collapsed, a cheap tent, between their torsos, both belly up. The sheet contained most of them, approximately sixty percent, crumpled up to their navels, covering his but not hers. Beads of sweat, absorbed by the sheet earlier, made it clammy, and so less soothing. The shaft of light that is caught by the metallic qualities in the body of the dilapidated typewriter cut across the bed at an acute angle of, say, fifty five degrees, catching her at the ankles and him in the shins. The wall, which is white and divides their basement room from the street, was refracting enough light to silhouette her upturned face without blackening in her features altogether. Her upper torso heaved and hoed slightly with her close, even breathing, as did his when he bothered to take notice. Uuuuupppp (pause) dddooownnn (pause), uuuuuppp (pause) dddooown. The words fit. The typewriter still had its a, e, and o ability. The applause could be for a piece of street theatre spoken from a place in the square which wouldn't allow the speaking to carry down the street through the window and into his ear, or perhaps the speakers simply had their backs toward him. The clappers would, in that case, be facing his ears. Two hundred people at least, four hundred hands. The resonance filled in its own gaps as it came and went, but occasionally started up and ended off a little messy. A game of tag, based on now you see me now you don't transfered from the eyes to the ears, audio displacement hide and seek, was using him as a makeshift vehicle and venue. The dark was happening to him while he lay still within it. A glow circumscribed the gray rectangle that hung in the window in the absence of a breeze and some of it entered the room. It was a representative of the illumination that was causing the old typewriter to shine. The far wall was almost completely invisible as was the chair she read in. He squinted in an effort to discern the outline of the chair and was successful, but he had to turn his head away from her to do so, so he returned it to its horizontal resting place. She — her close, even snoring, and her reading — was pacific, it lapped, he was on its beach, sprawled. The words fit. Up and down. Pausing. The pausing. He bathed in the pausing. Forgot everything but the pausing. Applause. Clapping, but now with a voice. A nearby voice. Now another, and not passing. Next door. Canned laughter. The voices stopped and turned off the applause. He heard the click. Bathos fell on him.

Lead bathos poured into the heat and began to crush him with its humid swaddling. The night had lied. The game was mockery. The canned laughter sucked back his square imaginings and left him high and silly. The dark was happening to him while floated within. A sinister glow surrounded the gray rectangle that hung in the window in the absence of a breeze and some of it invaded the room. The old typewriter was a deadly incandescent remainder. The victim's daughter snored even and close by his shoulder. Her face was dimly lit by just enough glow for him to recognize his chance. Pathos bubbled from him. Salty pathos, her reading, his message and risk became the air, her loud expiration his mute aspiration. Vehicle and venue. The night, she, and the mocking applause were making a game of his wakefulness. He began to surface into what contained him. He saw the night's need of him and looked more closely at the shine in the dilapidated body of the typewriter they'd found in an alley nearby. He remembered its a, e and o ability. The shaft of light which cut across his shin made her stomach amber. He had to kiss it, nothing else mattered. He could move. The night couldn't hold him. The humidity let him slip. Pathos surrendered, became sweat. He mopped his brow with his palm. Soaked in his body's juices, he glistened in the shaft of light preparing his lips. As his body passed across it, the shaft of light jumped on him and glistened, the room flickered, no, winked. So he dreamed love as a game of insomnia.

∘ *Waking* ∘

Perpendicular to him, and attached, she cantered into morning, her arms raised above her head but bent at the elbows, the first finger of her right hand preserving her place, her head back allowing what hair she had to hang, in accordance with gravity, down on her shoulders. Occasionally, in the early part of the day, she found it difficult to read. She'd moistened, and he'd marginally increased making copulative commotion merciful, but no less confounding to the necessary eye/word marriage of comprehension. The two parts, the read and the unread, held her finger in their papyrus gums like a weary ferret, her hand its prehensile jaw. His hands held her hips, his thumbs pointing to the protuberances which her head fell away from. Gyrations beyond either of them ran their course, melting them away and pouring them back again, but tuned to faint faraway psychic and synoptic stations. The voices passing in the street were oblivion overheard. The curtains did not billow their pale green, so still was the day's first light which managed to illuminate the room about ten watts worth with a fabricated, almost invisible, sea-water lime. She'd already seen the box but as she settled and sat, her gaze found it again and bid it a formal greeting. Its cardboard flaps were loosing their animate aspect. She was done with it but his mystery, his what next, held her in check. She would finish them, such as they were. The gesture was becoming fun. She decided to speak.

But as she was thinking this, leaning forward a little, rendering them acute of angle on their facewise axis, the axis upon which they had come to revolve, he was thinking something else and something else happened. Or, to be exact, what he thought happened. Or seemed to. And dramatically. Two figures waltzed in and began moving between door, window, and table, in a most graceful way, as prescribed, waltzed lightly, well. Was his ancestry playing up within? His thought reworded was, "The spectacle against which we are measured devolves us toward personal happiness. It treats us like Romans stinking of mothballs at a waltz, a masquerade of conviviality where Whimsy twirls Folly around and calls it Fun." It had been a finely tuned return from beyond either of them, need it be said, but surely this degree was surprising. By now she had, however, commenced her reading, saving him, for the minute, the exasperation of explanation. The conjured dancers were suitably bedecked, their gender in a noticeable uproar. The wench trim, the rogue dapper, both engrossed. The black masks they wore were held in place enchantingly by thin sticks which each ensconced with aptitude of consummate skill upon the other's very nose.

She had decided to speak when the book she held her finger in rose to her eyes like the fumes of dank, memorial macarones. She would finish them, such as they were — *Death Maze* by T.L. Barney, *Don Juan Does Detroit* by Ben T. Tucker, *A Calabash of Diamonds* by Seymour Hughes, and one other. The typewriter, which was dilapidated and somewhat dusty, stared, its remaining vowels still characters. The lino stood the floral trampling without redress. What the little blue ones were did not reach the assertive interrogative mode it might have hoped for. The curtains were billowed full of an odd first early wind and people going for baked goods noticed the twirling couple, their grace, and the lack of music. He was sweating, worried, and beginning to shrink from within her. Sudden company at such times could compromise a certain solace and sovereignty, he dared to think, but no untoward animation followed. At least she had the cover of words, the thraldom of the other worldly guise of superimposed context. Sweet William! Was it sweet William, that blue upon which the beautiful honed black toe of the left shoe of waltzing Whimsy—its, her, hair tied up and bowed by a ribbon of hot red satin— pivoted? Folly wore a white smoking jacket over a cream-coloured cashmere polo with a green carnation in the correct buttonhole of the lapel of the former and was nimble for its, his, age. The masks were more than costume consistent, that is, they were concealing certain correlations of identity and recognition. The typewriter was becoming impassive. Perhaps he would try without the missing to recount the maybe soon.

"The maybe soon," he said, but she was reading, brain keen deep in a *A Calabash of Diamonds* by Seymour Hughes, well beyond litany and waking. The waltzers began humming. What was she petitioning? Surely she knew they were the sum of what they couldn't tell each other. Two halves of a cheddar-round without the grain to match their severance. No empty air pockets to align, just boundless, borderless mutual silence. A breeze. The pale green curtains wiggled and the aquarium they, he, she (the reader), and their sudden company, swam in, quivered, its sea green ambrosia shimmering as if trying to convince itself it was real. The table was full of banquet, frugal but pure. Its sweating helped the cheese sparkle, this despite the mean ratio of photons to sable. She wasn't budging, and seemed not to notice the dancers. Or was she ignoring them? Denying them? Perhaps she is uncomfortable with Whimsy and unaware that Incarceration is its sole detractor. Perhaps she's jealous of Folly's swirl? He was unsure. Troy was a marriage of walls and space. She read on and began to dwindle. Whimsy's gown was an argument between the delicious and the ghastly, its face classical, divine, its bosom boyish. Folly uttered. They'd spun back from the corner where the cardboard box was flapping motionless, frozen framed, fast shutter photoed, when it (male voice in middle bass range) entoned,

"Don't mind us
Don't get up
Do please drain
Thy loving cup"
The rectangular stain on the wall facing him past the window

was visible now and leapt forward hot on the heels of this witty reassurance. It seemed to be of two minds, therefore offering contrary interpretations. One, aware of its debt to the picture, long since removed ("Do you mind?" her only words) and to which it owed its existence, if not its form, was still a little nonplussed by its blank interior and counselled embarrassment. The other, proud of its unveiling, pregnant with suggestions of what it might call itself, might so much as mean, advised amusement and a pithy rebuttal, something leaning in the direction of fount, fecundity, fission faddle, fon, and even uneven rhetoric.

She heard the ten words and two "don'ts" and, as if they were written into the text she was then part of, smiled at the timely wit with which they were inserted. Who would have expected such drollery of a police inspector attempting to hound clues from a recondite keeper of public drinking. Her amusement amused him and swayed his reaction in the direction of the rectangular stain's second interpretation, minus the verve. The typewriter was about to complain of its lack of ability to complain, in and of itself, that is without fingers' force and papyrus recorder, about the way these shameless showoffs prancing around, mocking its inability to complain, made it feel. The cheese was still trying to sparkle, and getting better at it too. Morning offered a few more photons every second second and the curtains' green influence, its message in an aquarium bottle, was thus gradually undermined. The waltzers, spinning swiftly across the room in the direction of her litanous cardboard cache, had come very wrapped up with each other or, at least based on his gaze, which was only briefly removed from their odd appearance, it seemed so. The aforementioned counsel of the far walls' rectangular stain, a record of pictorial absence, the picture by Vermeer that had inspired her only words—"Do you mind?"—was responsible for these brief removes of attention. This mood of complete self-regard distanced the dancers with such power that they became bizarre, almost hallucinatory, and somehow endearing. He did not question himself concerning his need to counsel the far wall's stain. In any event any retort would now be out of context, would disturb the comely wraiths. Meanwhile the flowers were opening, so to speak, were finding reward for their

patience with the coming of light to their perennial if scuffed and
faded pigment. Sweet William. He must ask someone if those little
blue ones were Sweet Williams. Or Corn Flowers? Whimsy or
Incarceration? The softness between her (its) mask and gown spoke
the tongue of passion, of all or nothing. He was thinking of siding
with "all," her all, with enchantment, when the concierge appeared
in the doorway and people at the window. They pushed the curtains
aside and climbed through at the gestured bequest of Folly in a
cream-coloured whirl. A small group is assembled and gaiety rules
their milling, their vibrant circulation. She hops up, bounds over to
the cardboard box, unflaps its ears and passes books out to the
astounded gathering. Some pair off and join the waltzers as passing
musicians take tuneful positions on the windowsill, some examine
what they've been handed by flicking through the pages as if
considering purchase, while others gawk and chatter mainly about
these exposed lives, inventing for them sequences of happiness or
despair. He goes to the anxious typewriter that hasn't all its
prescribed potential to bring fingertips to tip of tongue. The softness between mask and gown swoops past his ear. His Uncle's
message was a mad prank. It couldn't have saved her even if he'd
arrived in time. The coroner's report is vague, fanciful. She is
reading again in a huddle on the bed. A frenzy is unhatching and the
rectangular stain on the wall left by the absence of the censored
Vermeer is of two minds what to do about it. He must manage the
message before she goes. A stifling smell of flowers jumps up his
nose. Could it be the linoleum? He must deliver this message. It is
required before she dissolves into you altogether. He must deliver
the message of his blood. A stifling smell of flowers is deranging
his thoughts. Could it be Whimsy and the softness between mask
and gown swooping past his nostrils? They dip. It's a tango now.
Frenzy is unfolding at his back. They dip and Folly asks, "Why
d'you kill her?" The coroner's report was baffling. Can television
kill? Can sheer entertainment? Considered physiologically? She
died in his arms. His Uncle was mad, the message must be a prank,
how could it have saved her? "Why d'you kill her?" "If we found
you, so will they?" "We're only curious." "We're on your side."
"Gods." They begin to applaud. Why are they applauding? Stop

them applauding. This isn't Funny. He must write a message with less vowels than is prescribed by history. They continue applauding. She is dissolving into you. The tongue of all or nothing is dissolving into you. The smell of the linoleum is dissolving into you. The dancers are dissolving.

FICTION NORTH

MICHAEL CUNNINGHAM

GARY INDIANA

PATRICK McGRATH

EILEEN MYLES

LYNNE TILLMAN

WENDY WALKER

from *A Home at the End of the World*

Michael Cunningham

I never expected this, a love so ravenous it's barely personal.
A love that displaces you, pushes you out of shape. I knew that if
I was crossing the street with the baby and a car screamed around
the corner, horn blaring, I'd shield her with my body. I'd do it
automatically, the way you protect your head or heart by holding up
your arms. You defend your vital parts with your tougher, more
expendable ones. In that way, motherhood worked as promised.
But I found that I loved her without a true sense of charity or
goodwill. It was a howling, floodlit love; a frightening thing. I
would shield her from a speeding car but I'd curse her as I did it, like
a prisoner cursing the executioner.

Rebecca's mouth worked to form the word "Momma." She
fretted whenever I left her. Someday she'd pay a fortune to
therapists for their help in solving the mystery of my personality.
There would be plenty of material—a mother living with two
men, intricately in love with both of them. An undecided,
disorganized woman who fell out of every conventional
arrangement. Who dragged her own childhood along with
her into her forties. I'd been just a private, slipshod person
going about my business and now I was on my way to
becoming the central riddle in another person's life.

Being a mother was the weighted, unsettling thing. Being a
lover—even an unorthodox lover—was tame and ordinary by
comparison.

Maybe that was the secret my own mother discovered. She'd
thought my wild, undisciplined father would prove to be her life's
adventure. And then she'd given birth.

We worked out a variation on the classic arrangement, we

three. Bobby and Jonathan went to the cafe before sunrise every morning, I stayed home with Rebecca. I didn't want a business. Eventually I'd start making jewelry again, or some other little thing. The restaurant was the boys' project, a way for them to support themselves and begin paying me back. They were good, uncomplaining workers. Or, Bobby was a good, uncomplaining worker and Jonathan more or less followed his example. They left the house at five o'clock every morning, just as the darkness was beginning to turn, and didn't come back until four or five in the afternoon, when the dark was already working its way back into the corners of the house. To be honest, I didn't know too much about their work lives. Bobby cooked, Jonathan was the waiter, and a sweet dim-witted boy from town bussed tables and did the dishes. Although I listened to their stories—furious customers, kitchen fixtures that blew up or caught fire in the middle of the lunch rush, wildly improbable thefts (someone stole the stuffed salmon right off the wall, someone else took the seat off the toilet in the women's room)—it all seemed to happen in a remote, slightly unliving realm of anecdote. I felt for the boys. But to me their single, salient characteristic was an eleven- or twelve-hour daily absence. Real life, the heart and heft of it, was what happened during the hours they were gone.

For years, for most of my recollected life, I'd walked carefully over a subterranean well of boredom and hopelessness that lay just beneath the thin outer layer of my imagination. If I'd stood still too long, if I'd given in to repose, I'd have fallen through. So I'd made things, gone to clubs and movies. I'd kept changing my hair.

Now, with Rebecca to care for, each moment had an electrified gravity that was not always pleasant but ran right down to the core. Sometimes I grew bored—babies aren't always interesting—but always, in another minute or hour, she would need something only I could provide. It seemed that every day she developed a new gesture or response that carried her that much closer to her own eventual personality. From hour to hour, she kept turning more fully into somebody. The hours were stitched together, and nothing limp or hopeless ever threatened to unravel the day. I bathed Rebecca, fed her, mopped up her shit. I played with her. I showed her what I could of the world.

All right, I liked it best when the boys were gone. Once they came home, a sense of continuing emergency was lost. Weary as they were, they told me to relax while they attended to Rebecca. They were being good, responsible fathers. I knew I should feel appreciative. But I didn't want to relax. I wanted to be stretched and beset. I wanted to be frantically busy with Rebecca every waking moment, and then fall into a sleep black and shapeless as the unlived future.

Bobby loved our daughter but was not tormented by her vulnerable, noisy existence. In a world with more room in it he might have been a settler, with visions of reinventing society on a patch of ground far from the site of the old mistakes. He had that religious quality. He was soft-hearted and intensely focused. He was not deeply interested in the flesh. Sometimes when he held Rebecca I knew how he saw her—as a citizen in his future world. He respected her for swelling the local population but did not agonize over particulars of her fate. In his eyes, she was part of a movement.

Bobby and I slept together in a new queen-size bed. Rebecca's room was the next down the hall, followed by the bathroom and Jonathan's room. Bobby's days were unrelenting. He flipped eggs and baked pies, fought with suppliers. He came home to Rebecca's cries and dirty diapers. At night he slept the sleep of the exhausted and depleted—a desperate unconsciousness. I was grateful for his waning interest in sex, not only because I was tired also but because my nipples had turned brown from Rebecca's nursing. Three yellow stretch marks stitched their way from my bottom rib to my crotch. I was forty-one. I couldn't feel pretty anymore. If Bobby had been more ardent or high-strung, if he'd shamefacedly confessed that I repelled him now, I'd have had something to work from. I might have started on a new kind of defiant pride. But he was himself, a charitable, hardworking man. We slept peacefully together.

Jonathan generated more static electricity as he ran through his days. If Bobby moved with the methodical, slightly bovine will of a vacuum cleaner, sucking up each errand and task, Jonathan clattered along like an eggbeater. He was manic and flushed, vague-eyed from lack of rest. He and Bobby both told me that, as a waiter, he offered charm in place of competence. Water glasses went unfilled. Eggs ordered scrambled arrived sunnyside up. He said there were moments during the breakfast rush when he actually seemed to fall asleep while moving. One moment he'd be filling a cream pitcher and the next he'd be standing beside a table, in the middle of taking an order, with no recollection of the intervening time. Soon he and Bobby would hire a waitress, and Jonathan would become the host and backup errand boy. "I'll make sure everybody's happy," he said. "I'll pour them more coffee and ask about their hometowns. We'll hire a specialist to see that they actually get what they order."

His true vocation was the baby. Every evening after work he brought her something: a plastic doll from the dime store, a rose from somebody's garden, a pair of miniature white sunglasses. He took her for long walks before dinner and read to her after.

Around four in the morning he'd wake her, change her diaper, and bring her to Bobby's and my bed. He was comically paternal in boxer shorts, carrying our sleepy child. "I know it borders on child abuse, getting her up like this," he said. "But we need to see her before we go off to bake the bread." He'd crawl into bed beside me, holding Rebecca on his lap. Some mornings she whined sleepily in the lamplight. Some mornings she chuckled and mouthed unintel-ligible words. "Miss Rebecca," Jonathan would whisper. "Oh, you're a fine thing, aren't you? Mm-hm. Oh yes. Look at those hands. You'll be a tennis player, huh? Or a violinist, or a human fly." He kept up a stream of talk, an unwavering flow. Sometimes when she cried, only Jonathan could comfort her. She'd wail in my arms, and buck and shriek in Bobby's. But when Jonathan took her she'd quiet down. She'd stare at him with eyes that were greedy and surprisingly hard. She clung to him because he was elusive and because, during his hours at home, he took the most elaborate, courtly care of her. Even that early, I believe she was falling in love.

Rebecca and I shared a more nervous kind of love. While the

boys were away, she and I lived together in a state of constant need. She needed and, with growing vehemence, resented my protection. I only needed her safety but I needed it completely, all the time. I had to know she was all right, every minute. It took its toll on both of us.

Sometimes when we were together, when I checked the temperature of her bathwater or snatched a pencil out of her mouth, I could almost feel the question crackling in the air around us— *What if I fail to protect?* We could grow irritable together. I could be short-tempered with her, and bossy; I could deny her too much. She was addicted to my fears. She wept if I watched her too closely, and wept if she realized that for a moment I'd forgotten to watch her at all.

I was beginning to understand something about my mother. She'd made a choice after I was born. There wasn't room in the house or in her parsimonious nature for two difficult children. She'd been forced to choose. Maybe that was how the battle started. My father had had to fight for a share. He'd used his best weapons, his sex and recklessness, but my mother had prevailed with her powers of organization and rectitude. I'd loved my father more. He'd called me Peg and Scarlett O'Hara, said it was all right to buy anything we wanted. But toward the end, when he fell cursing on the front lawn and drunkenly broke furniture, I'd turned away from him. Finally, a child will choose order over passion or charm.

As a grown woman I'd fallen in love with Jonathan's intelligence and humor and, I suppose, with his harmlessness. He was neither frigid nor dangerous. Neither man nor woman. There was no threat of failure through sex. Now I saw how Rebecca, too, would one day fall in love with him. He had a father's allure. He had a mother's warmth without the implied threat—she would not die if Jonathan briefly lost track of her. He worked all day and then came home with a present in his hands, flushed with the sheer excitement of seeing her after so many hours' separation. Bobby was sweetly remote and I was too constant. Jonathan exerted a steady charm made perfect by his daily absence. Rebecca would be his. She'd care for Bobby and me but she'd belong to Jonathan.

There were times—moments—when I believed I had in fact

found my reward. I had love, and a place on earth. I was part of something sweetened and buffered. A family. It was what I'd thought I wanted. My own family had crackled with jealousy and rage. Not a single one of my parents' wedding gifts survived. We'd devoured the past. Now nothing was left to inherit but the improvements my mother had made, the gilt fixtures and floral prints, after my father went off to quit drinking and find Christ and then start drinking again.

But at other times I missed the violent wrongheadedness of my own family. We'd been difficult people, known around the neighborhood: Poor Amelia Stuckart and That Man She Married. I'd grown famous in our suburb for being Their Poor Little Girl. I'd based my early self-inventions on the concepts of deprivation and pride. I'd worn the shortest skirts, teased my hair into a brittle storm. I'd fucked my first skinny bass player at fourteen, in the back of a van. The local forces of order made it easy for me by wearing lumpy bras and girlish hairdos, by slathering their jowls with Aqua Velva. They said, "Join us in our world," and I found a drug dealer for a boyfriend. I watched myself shrink in the eyes of the counselors and the pastors—*perhaps, in fact, Mrs. Rollins, this one is beyond our help.* I went to school with a pint of tequila in my purse. I shot through the frozen Rhode Island nights sizzling on speed. I left a vapor trail behind. People who've been well cared for can't imagine the freedom there is in being bad.

Now, late in life, I'd been rescued. The boys came straight home every night, took care of Rebecca, cooked our dinner. Their love wasn't immaculate. They may have loved one another more than they loved me. They may have been using me without quite knowing it. I could live with that. I didn't mind touching the rough bottom of people's good intentions. What I had trouble with sometimes was the simple friendliness of it. We lived in a world of kindness and domestic order. I sometimes thought of myself as Snow White living among the dwarfs. The dwarfs took good care of her. But how long would she have lasted there without the hope of meeting someone life-sized? How long would she have swept and mended before she began to see her life as composed of safe haven and subtle but pervasive lacks?

From *The Fever*

Gary Indiana

But let me tell you about another, even more curious adventure.

I was living in Munich with Gilda and Klaus, in an apartment on Herzogstrasse, Schwabing, between the University and Muenchener Freiheit. In a storage closet, amid hanging bales of plastic dry-cleaning bags, with one suitcase, the soft green one, full of dirty laundry. It was July, hot, boring, the atmosphere tense, vaguely mistrustful, irritating...and Gilda's clothes, draped around the narrow folding bed like ghosts of a scene that had come and gone.

I lay awake in the night, the moonlight through the transom window throwing spindly shadows overhead, convinced that parts of my body had taken on an independent life. My hands seemed too thick and willful for my arms, my feet squirmed rebelliously against my ankles, my ears scraped the pillow like alien append-ages. I was thirty years old. Nothing I had ever done had amounted to anything. I smoked a cigarette in the dark and contemplated my options. I had none.

It all had to do with Fuchs, whom I had encountered in New York the previous winter, phoning me at erratic intervals concern-ing his plans, big plans, something to do with film production. Fuchs was unhappy with the roles he was getting offered in Germany. He would produce his own movies from now on, with huge starring parts for himself, and what did I think about it? I had had some experiences in the theater. Fuchs thought perhaps...with an American collaborator...and now this apartment, inhabited by vague acquaintances...clean, that eerie cleanliness so common in Germany. Nervous, frightened cleanliness. I sat up. I flicked on the overhead light. I counted the bundle of money in my suitcase. There was absolutely no hope of more money except through Fuchs, who was turning out to be...recalcitrant, to put it mildly....

Klaus's old shoes, Gilda's dresses, the cigarette end, the shrinking bundle of marks, my fingers...what could it possibly mean? And what on earth would come of it? Gilda and Klaus...it was impossible to tell what their relationship was, or what had brought them together. Gilda worked in a mental clinic in Starnberg, performing "arts and crafts rehabilitation" on various schizophrenics. Klaus had some sort of permanent depressive damage from his family, his father's ugly past, unregenerated Nazi cousins and uncles and other Bavarians from Alter Pfarrhof, "where Catholicism waves its brainless sceptre." They were hospitable enough, quick with apologies for improbable slights, prone to melancholic staring into space...like traumatized rabbits.

Gilda drove to the asylum a few mornings a week, in polite muted plaids, sweater sets, flat shoes, hair tortured into a cork-colored bun, dash of pale pink lipstick, her pretty round face a mask of subdued anxiety. At night she tore off her work clothes as if they'd gotten contaminated, stood under cold showers, let her hair down, slipped into vivid dresses and a "vivacious" personality full of obvious desperation. As for Klaus, he...painted, the same painting every day, in different colors. One per day, exactly the same sixteen inch square format, a cross, green on gray background, or red on white, or yellow on blue, pewter on lavender, rust on orchid pink, Klaus had a system, it was all carefully recorded in a thick ledger, typewritten inventories...with precise, abstemious notes on what he'd eaten that day, what time he went to bed, what the weather had been....

Their days were brisk and organized and gave the feeling of a large clock motoring inexorably in the background. A week passed, then another week, and then one morning Klaus stepped out for a quart of milk. Dappled sunlight poured into the gray kitchen through the limbs of a diseased elm in the back yard. Gilda stood at the cutting board spreading duck pâté on a wedge of toast. She held the knife up to look at it and said:

"He'd go nuts, if he didn't control himself...his father! Imagine! The man operated the gas chambers! He did the selections! When the Jews came off the cattle cars, his father was right there! And now this monster is a tourist guide at Dachau!"

There was an abrupt silence. Gilda resumed slathering the toast with meat paste, set it down on a plate, and poured coffee into three mugs, with a rueful pout. She sat down, spooned sugar into her mug, and smiled, as if nothing at all had happened. We heard Klaus's keys in the door, his footsteps on the parquet in the hall, and then Gilda was pouring milk into a little china pitcher, Klaus regaled us with some queer incident at the corner shop, I chimed in with something similar that had happened to me the day before, Gilda glanced at her watch, Klaus lit a cigarette, and so on.

A few days later, I saw Klaus browsing through the philosophy section of the university bookstore. Leibnitz, of all things. Is there a metaphysical reason why the world should exist, just as it is rather than otherwise? Did I feel like a drink? We walked through the unconvincing sidewalk cafes on Leopoldstrasse, past the big movie theaters, to a beer cellar full of large, loud, middleaged men with puffy faces. Klaus drank several peppermint schnapps. He surveyed the gray, smoky room, licked schnapps from his lips, and expropriated one of my cigarettes.

"Gilda's father, you know, is on the board of I.G. Farben. All through the war years, and still, now, without a minute's interruption. He's all denazified and rich as a sultan. When the Baader people were operating in Munich, she tried to persuade them to bump him off. He wasn't important enough."

"She really wanted him murdered?"

"No, executed. For political crime. Absolutely. She even bought a pistol, or maybe stole it from his house, which she still has. You've seen that little safe in her room? I think she's worried I might...well, I've thought about it, it's true. But I'd never do it in the apartment. Sometimes after a suicide, the police tear through everything, and she keeps a little cocaine in there, too. Only a small amount, but the law is very strict in Bavaria. Anyway, I wouldn't shoot myself. I detest guns, they leave such a mess. Ready for another beer?"

As far as Fuchs was concerned, it was obvious that this well-known actor had stopped getting work because his weight doubled by the week. He had eaten himself out of a job. Gluttony was affecting his brain, too. Willie, known also as Lily to the movie swells, had established a production office in a trucking garage on Turkenstrasse with a lot of borrowed money. The company had churned out a splatter film on a plantation in the Philippines, and now they were shooting a light comedy about film extras at a studio in Haar. Fuchs and his associates were mostly known from the gritty social dramas of the "genius," Rudolph Zryd. They were rabid for a commercial hit, anything that would bring the bucks in. The company's development schedule was crammed with Westerns, sentimental melodramas, horror films...the lower the tone, the better...but none of them, least of all Fuchs, had the foggiest instinct for formula. The scripts were churned out by an assortment of drunkards and hangers-on, bit players, and film students working on their doctorates.

Fuchs had asked me to slough through a pile of these scripts. "They're all shit," I told him. "Makes no difference," Fuchs insisted. "We'll sell it to television." Even the television had turned down his plantation epic, however. It only screened as a novelty item at festivals in Australia and South America. That suited Fuchs well enough, really. Free air tickets and hotels, banquets, receptions, sexual opportunities, exotica: Fuchs had a gift for wheedling these perks from all over the world. I had met him, in fact, at a film retrospective that Fuchs had mooched out of a German cultural organization in New York.

Epicene, with pudgy brown ringlets that garnished the spreading angelic face of an inflatable putti, Fuchs had played sweet, duped husbands, child molesters, and softheaded aristocrats in dozens of art films. Only Rudolph Zryd, the "genius," had thought to cast Fuchs as an oily working-class pouf in tasteless blazers and scarves, an inveterate, more or less invertebrate gossip, air-brain, and petty opportunist with no moral sense. Fuchs was larger than that, in every sense, but he did have the germs of his characters embedded somewhere in his overweight soul.

It was a dreary, stagnant time in Munich. Years had passed since the Stammheim "suicides." Bavaria was a sleepy, disillusioned duchy, under the fascist dinosaur Strauss. U-bahn stations and supermarkets featured wanted posters of youthful, attractive terrorists. Fuchs took me to lunch two or three times a week, usually to a restaurant in the suburbs, for what he termed a business meeting. But always, first, there was a great deal of standing or sitting around his office, upstairs in the trucking warehouse. Down below, crates of film equipment and scaffolding and painted sets wheeled in and out of the courtyard.

I found him wedged in a squishy leather desk chair, glazed eyes obscured by reading spectacles, glowering moistly into vacant space. Through a grid of dirty panes behind his head, monotonous treetops and cowering tile roofs extended for miles under a seablue sky. Across the street, a steam shovel bit into debris from a condemned block of flats, conveyed messy iron mouthfuls to a fleet of yellow dumpsters. A single, slender glass tower pierced the peripheral view, capped by a colossal neon Mercedez hood ornament.

Jammed deep in Fuchs's ear was the olive Bakelite receiver of the desk phone. He chewed a lead pencil, lustfully. In fitful reverie his next meal was forming on the banquette of his imagination.

"My dear friend...payments went out three weeks ago. I'm certain...no...I don't have the check in front of me...turnover in the department...misfiled, possibly...when people leave, there's carelessness...exactly...."

Fuchs's bulging blue eyes rolled, his lower lip sagged ponderously, his expression begged: "Does this idiot believe me?" He massaged his breasts through his shirt, lit innumerable cigarettes, attached pencils and paper clips and map tacks to strips of scotch tape and dangled them from his sausage digits. He fastened a damp palm to the mouthpiece and ejected a strident, baritone fart. As he resumed talking he fanned the air with the desk blotter after sweeping myriad loose objects from it with his forearm. Fuchs burlesqued asphyxiation while rasping figures into the phone.

There were brisk movements in the hall outside. A ladder, a secretary, a workman dragging a large wooden cutout somewhere, a boy in brown overalls shouldering a case of Pepsi. Out the window, the steam shovel had frozen with its hydraulic elbow in midair. A breeze shook the treetops. An actor whose face I recognized from Zryd's movies looked in for a moment, Fuchs growled something in German, the actor slapped his forehead, the secretary brushed past him, dumped a clipboard full of papers on Fuchs's desk, and went out again, brushing lint from her skirt. Fuchs hung up the phone and staggered to his feet.

"My dear friend," he declared without irony, "everyone wants a piece of me."

Behind the wheel of his new but extremely grimy subcompact, the kind with a million control buttons embedded in the dashboard and shoulder straps that automatically slap themselves across the torso and entangle the passenger, Fuchs abandoned himself to childishness. He played with the windows, the windshield wipers, fiddled with the radio, cut off other cars at intersections, raced lights, screamed obscenities at pedestrians, gave himself a mint, fooled with a pair of sunglasses, belched, picked his nose, lit cigarettes, tossed litter out the window, whistled, sang, scratched his head, sucked his knuckles, bit his nails, and generally wallowed in his Fuchsness.

"Here's a story idea," he announced, ripping open a giant bar of chocolate against the steering wheel. "It's called 'The Music Teacher,' or something like that...piece of candy? No? That's your trouble, you know, you don't eat...our story takes place in Japan, but now that I think about it, it could be Munich, too... The music teacher is a beautiful woman who is, unfortunately, blind, thanks to a childhood illness, at first she's sent to a music master, to learn...what is that instrument, I forget what...the lute?...anyway...in time, he realizes her gift is greater than his own, and later, he becomes her pupil.... He devotes his life to her. He becomes her slave, in a sense.

"Others, naturally, are jealous...because Miyoki, or whatever her name is...is so much admired...always giving recitals, and getting all the rich pupils...and anyway, she's spoiled, very selfish, mistreats the students and so on...and one night, her lover, her slave, hears her cry out, he hurries to her room, and there finds that someone has thrown boiling water in her face, yes? And now her beauty is ruined. He drives nails into his own eyes, so he will never see her as mutilated."

"This sounds very familiar, Willie."

"Well, like many Oriental tales, isn't it?"

"More like one particular Oriental tale, actually."

Fuchs was nothing if not shameless.

"Really? Which one?"

Fuchs had a fascination for cruelty and cruel stories. It was a characteristic of his crowd, the Zryd crowd, to pride themselves on a certain Teutonic iron in the soul. Fuchs was Austrian, of course, so the iron was smothered in whipped cream and marzipan. Your father died? Ha ha, too bad. Bankrupt? Tough luck! Cancer? Well, life is hard, only the strong survive. He owed me a great deal of money. Between bursts of pointless conversation an emphatic silence trickled into the car.

He knew I needed cash, and fumbled around desperately for evasive chatter. "He's never going to pay me," I thought, and wondered why it surprised me. Perhaps because Fuchs had the actor's gift of seeming loveable against all evidence to the contrary.

For a previous luncheon surprise, Willie had treated me to boiled beef and shredded cabbage at an extremely brown tavern which he said had been a tremendous favorite of Adolf Hitler. We had watched two ancient truck farmers shooting billiards, spitting on the floor, and gulping huge tankards of pilsner. Willie had encouraged the octogenarian waiter's reminiscences, which involved serving macaroni to the Fuhrer shortly before the Beer Hall Putsch of 1923.

We drove across Munich, to a white frame house on a quiet street, where a trellised walk led to a woodsy rear garden. A dozen tables dotted a fieldstone terrace. Fuchs swobbed perspiration from his face with his napkin. When he relaxed his professional physiognomy, it softened into hapless, vulnerable shiftiness, only vaguely mammalian, as if his enormity made strictly human expressions impossible to maintain. He mutated into a whale, or a boar, or an undifferentiated mass of gristle...his red mouth with its gasping rictus, his little teeth marooned in their wads of pale gum, his hair frizzling in the humidity.... A waiter filled the water glasses. A number of small, tawny birds flittered between a grape arbor and the fieldstones, pecking crumbs. Fuchs fished out a cigarette pack, straightened a crumpled cigarette, and smiled stupidly as he lit it. The heat made everything swarm and melt into nothing.

"A bottle of Riesling? Fine, wunderbar…and why don't you like my music teacher idea? I'm evaporating in this heat, look at this shirt! Anyway, it doesn't matter. I have another idea. By the way, you must try the pork schnitzel, it's delicious here…all the famous people come here. You don't get this nice kind of place setting in Munich, with the heavy flatware and so on. And the little birds, so beautiful…doesn't it give you a feeling of peace? It reminds me of my childhood and its endless summer days. What has happened to Little Willie, I often wonder? Where is that little boy who delighted to watch the clouds, and the birds…."

Dumpling soup arrived. The little boy who had delighted to watch the clouds and the birds polished it off in seconds, along with the contents of a generous bread basket. He waved for the waiter. He wanted…another soup, right away, before the main course. As he ingurgitated everything within reach…wine, bread, a small bowl of olives…Fuchs expounded his latest dream, a stage extravaganza written just for him. All singing, all dancing. Yes, dancing, what did I think, that just because his weight—? It was true, Fuchs had an angelic singing voice, and was light on his toes, too, for someone weighing as much as a small automobile. And I could write it for him!

"If you do this for me, seriously…we could entirely solve this money problem of yours…you don't mind?" His fork plunged into my soup bowl, spearing the half-eaten dumpling. "It has to be racy! Like a burlesque, but more explicit. With nudity! Don't look at me like that…nudity of young people, in the background! While I dance and sing! In this show we explore every type of sexuality: gay, straight, with animals, necrophilia, domination, masturbation—all sex! Something that will outrage people! But also, we must charm them, you see, there has to be tenderness…and love…."

The schnitzel appeared, another bottle of wine, some vegetables. And mashed potatoes. The waiter's hairy hands, the hopping sparrows, a breeze soughing through the cypresses, a woman at another table coughing, shreds of nearby conversation, all in

German, a green bottle of mineral water, a lump of butter melting in a dish. Fuchs chewed through everything with sinister joie de vivre. I thought: I could always go to Paris and visit Clarice, or wire my bank for the rest of my savings....

"Not going to eat that? You never eat your meal, that's why you look so unhappy all the time. You take things too seriously. My philosophy, if you must know: eat the best food you can find, drink the nicest wine, live today like you will be dead tomorrow. Problems will sort themselves out."

I tried to imagine Fuchs naked, on a stage. I couldn't. As he ate, Fuchs's face filled with an expression of...diabolical energy, delusional optimism, insane self-assurance.... But invariably, metabolically, Fuchs could not sustain his bright chatter and his prodigious plans, once his demand for food had been satiated he became torpid, like a boa constrictor...and depressed, sullen, unresponsive....

Coffee was served. Fuchs asked for a cognac. He stubbed out one cigarette and lit another. A tiny bird landed on the table, caught a plug of bread in its beak, flew off. Fuchs was sliding into the depths. A mountain of lard, staring at the tablecloth, his face turning oily and pale like a slice of Emmenthaler cheese. I asked him a question. Fuchs continued staring at his fingers on the table. He was thinking deep, moody thoughts about his crummy childhood in Vienna, or his weight, or God knew what....

"Shit," he said finally.

"I beg your pardon?"

"Shit, I said. This is shit, I have another appointment...right away! I'm already late...I'll drop you in town, I must make some arrangements...about the movie, some leasing papers have to be signed, for the lights.... Now, look, about this money business, I have absolutely no money available today, maybe not for another week. It may look like I have, but at this moment I am living on credit, no lie.... Think about this famous sex show! All kinds of sex! I'll tell you what, write for me a few scenes, with a song or two, and in a few days.... Well, I'll get some money from somewhere, I can pay you two or three hundred marks...but only if it's good! Twenty marks, and five and five is thirty...my dear, do you have any small money for the tip?"

from *The Spider*

Patrick McGrath

Hilda was a prostitute, you see. She was a tart, and she paid my father with the services of a tart, though he didn't realize it until that night in the alley. When he got home half an hour later—he had smoked a cigarette by the canal, despite the cold of the night—he found to his annoyance that my mother was waiting up for him. I heard his boots in the yard, and then I heard him come in through the back door. My mother was sitting at the kitchen table in the dark, with a cup of tea, and he did not see her until he switched the light on. Her face, as she turned toward him, was puffy around the eyes, the way it got when she had been crying. "Still up?" he muttered as he sat down heavily at the other end of the table and bent to unlace his boots. He could not look at her.

"Where have you been, Horace?" she said quietly. There was a trace of accusation in her voice, accusation tempered with misery. The door from the kitchen into the passage was open, so I crept out of bed (I'd only been home a short while myself) and sat at the top of the stairs, in my pajamas, to listen. Did my father, even at this stage, have any decency at all left in him? Did her unhappiness catch at his heart and tear him, tear him between an involuntary spurt of compassion for my mother, for whose pain he alone was responsible—and his intense irritation with her, not only because she was a hindrance to him in his tawdry affair with Hilda Wilkinson but also because she complicated the clean hard thrust of his desire? His heart was not yet completely turned to stone, I believe; she aroused in him still, I think, traces of the responsibility he'd once felt for her, but the guilt triggered by these feelings he was forced violently to suppress, and for one simple reason: he could maintain his lust for Hilda only if he simultaneously hardened himself against my mother—if, in other words, he made a sort of unnatural

compartmentalization of his emotions: the only alternative was to
flounder about in muddle and indecision, a flaccid, unmanly condition he was anxious to avoid. So while one tiny voice cried out to
him to comfort my mother, to wipe away the tears from those bleary
eyes, take her in his arms and make everything all right again—an
opposite and equal impulse told him to make her suffer, intensify
the crisis, provoke the breakdown and dissolution of whatever
frayed bonds still held them together. So he did not comfort her, he
set his jaw in a thin, hard line, pulled off his boots, one by one, and
rubbed his feet. "Down the pub," he said.

"Down the Dog?"

"Yes."

"Liar! You're a liar, Horace!" she cried. Oh, it was hard for
me to hear her voice cracking like that, she such a stranger to anger!
"I went down the Dog and you weren't there!" Now she was
sitting upright at the end of the table with the tears streaming
down and a sort of watery light gleaming in her eyes, fury and
misery combined.

"I went somewhere else after a bit," my father said angrily.
"What were you down the Dog for? It's not Saturday."

She didn't answer this, just sat there staring at him as the tears
came flooding down her cheeks, not even bothering to wipe them away.

My father shrugged, dropping his eyes and rubbing his feet
once more. "I went down the Earl of Rochester." I heard him say it,
and I thought, why would he tell her that? How could he go down
there again, with her likely to come looking for him? "What are you
chasing after me for?" he said angrily. "Can't a man have a drink
after his work?"

"I won't live like this," said my mother, quiet again after her
outburst, and wiping her face with her apron. "I wasn't meant to live
like this."

"That's not my fault," said my father, as a voice in his head
said: oh yes it is.

"Yes it is," said my mother, for an uncanny moment becoming the articulation of his conscience.

"It's not!" he shouted—and I could stand no more. Down the
stairs I pattered, along the passage, barefoot and feigning sleepiness.

My mother turned toward me, and the sight of her tear-streaked face upset me badly. "It's all right, Spider," she murmured, blinking once or twice as she rose wearily from the table and smoothed her apron across her stomach in that way she had. "Your father and me, we're just having a talk."

"You woke me up," I said, or something of the sort I don't remember exactly.

"It's all right now," she said again, "we're all coming to bed now." She took my hand; I was taller than her, even in my bare feet. "Come on, my big Spider," she said, "back up to bed," and up the stairs we went. My father sat there at the table for another ten minutes or so, then I heard him turn off the light and come upstairs. My mother was awake, lying on her back in that huge bed of theirs and staring at the ceiling; the glow from the streetlamp outside sifted through the curtains and created queer rhomboid grids of light and shadow overhead. My father undressed and climbed in on his side, and the pair of them lay there in the darkness, silent and sleepless, for more than an hour.

When my father rose the next morning, and dressed for work, and went downstairs, he found my mother at the kitchen stove frying bacon. She had laid a clean white cloth on the table and poured his tea. She was all quiet bustling activity; she broke a couple of eggs into the skillet and a moment later set the plate before him: bacon and eggs, fried tomato and fried kidneys. "I popped out and got you something nice for your breakfast," she said. "You need a good breakfast in the morning, you work hard." Then she cut three slices from a fresh loaf and smeared them with dripping for his lunch. My father ate his breakfast; he said nothing, but dead as he was he couldn't have been unaware of the meaning and quality of her gesture. "Drink your tea while it's hot," she murmured as she wrapped his sandwiches in newspaper. He left for work a few minutes later, out through the back door; I watched him from my bedroom window. She was at the sink as he went out, I heard the water running. He paused a moment in the doorway, and looked back at her. She gave him a small smile, without lifting her hands from the washing-up water, and he produced an expression about his mouth, a sort of squeezing together of the lips, that was part resignation, part regret; and then he nodded once or twice. Cycling to work in the sharp fresh early morning air I imagine him feeling oddly at peace; it was the night that brought the passion and the confusion and the pain, in the morning it was different. Several times over the course of the day he resolved to have done with Hilda Wilkinson altogether. He reminded himself of what she'd said to him the previous night, he remembered how much he disliked the people she drank with, and not least, he thought about the devastation of my mother, should she ever find out what was going on. That truly gave him pause; flaccid and unmanly it may have been, but *that* he was not prepared to face. No, this brief affair with Hilda Wilkinson, this brief encounter—best put it behind him, forget about it, return to the routines of everyday life, those stable routines that he'd known, so it seemed, forever.

My father's resolution remained firm until, I would guess, about the middle of the afternoon. He was overhauling the plumbing of a warehouse in East Ham with his mate Archie Boyle, a cheery fat youth with hair the color of a carrot. I see him on a wooden stepladder, his shins braced against the top step, working with hammer and wrench on a length of old lead piping high in the dust and the gloom. Every clang of his hammer echoes dully through the empty building, and over this reverberating clangor comes the sharp, thin sound, from down the other end, of Archie's whistling; he is at work preparing sections of new pipe for my father to install. In his left hand my father grips the wrench, which is locked upon an antiquated octagonal nut that over the years has fused with its pipes, and with the right he wields the hammer, and with it delivers a series of steady blows to the shank of the wrench, in an effort to loosen the nut. Each hammer blow resounds through the warehouse like the tolling of some awful funereal requiem bell, flakes of rust drift free, and he has to turn his head to keep them from getting in his eyes. Slowly the nut starts to turn. My father's mind, lulled by the steady dirgelike clangor of his hammer blows, superimposed, in that big empty chamber, like some sort of eerie

Gothic symphony, on the slow tuneless whistling of Archie Boyle, has drifted, again, to the events of last night, to the sight of Hilda with her coat pushed back, her hands on her hips, bare-legged, one knee crooked so her skirt rides up her white thigh, grinning her chinny grin from the shadows—and with that image the idea of having her, there in the alley, that *tart* (how he savors the word!), up against the wall, with her skirt pushed up round her waist—

Suddenly from out of the pipe leaps a great hissing spurt of cold water. It hits him square in the chest and almost knocks him off the ladder. From all around the loosened nut spring jets of hissing water—the pipes have not been shut off at the mains. Archie comes trotting down the warehouse as my father descends the ladder, dripping wet and cursing, while the water sprays the ceiling and the top of the wall, then runs down to form a spreading puddle on the concrete floor. "Bloody hell!" shouts my father as he strides away to shut off the water. He does not need to be told that this is his fault.

When he returns, Archie, still whistling, is hard at work with bucket and mop. No great problem, after all; but as my father angrily resumes work on the eight-sided nut he knows that if it hadn't been for Hilda this wouldn't have happened. The pair resume their tasks; but all the while, outside the dusty warehouse windows, the light is thickening in the bleak gray November afternoon; and as it thickens my father cannot keep his thoughts from turning, again and again, to Hilda, to his tart, and the longing comes back like a fever, and his resolutions are all forgotten.

Soon afterwards the two plumbers left the empty warehouse. With the descent of darkness a damp, chilly fog had drifted in from the river, and my father pulled his cap low and tied his scarf tightly about his throat. After parting with Archie he mounted his bicycle and pedaled off in the direction of Kitchener Street. The moisture of the fog gathered round his spectacles and made his eyes smart as through obscure, deserted streets he rode, past black walls that glistened slickly where they caught the diffuse glow of the streetlamps, then retreated once more into inky indistinctness. Occasionally a figure hurried by, the footsteps becoming suddenly loud then just as quickly receding into silence. My father's route carried him along streets that tended down toward the docks, and as it did so the fog became denser, the city more deserted, the atmosphere more eerily muffled. Chill and damp though the evening was, with the onset of darkness, and the fading of his morning's resolutions, my father's physical desire had grown stronger, and now he was flushed and distracted with it; he could no more remember his decision to end the affair than he could have risen on his bicycle over the roofs and chimneys of the East End and left the imperatives of the flesh beneath and behind him forever.

On he crawled through the dark drear fog, his body on fire with the longing for Hilda Wilkinson. It smoldered inside him like the molten coke at the heart of a forge, it burned and seethed in the fog so that by the time he wheeled his bicycle into the back yard of number twenty-seven he was a man diseased, a man in fever, no longer responsible for his actions.

He entered the kitchen. I've told you what this room was like, it was a poky, ill-lit room, and one would be hard-pressed to call it cosy. Nevertheless my mother had taken pains to render it warm and homelike. The curtains, as shabby and faded as her apron, were drawn across the grimy window over the sink, and from the stove issued the sizzle and odor of liver frying in onions. She had washed the dishes, swept the floor, and even brought in from the front parlor her only plant, a wilted and failing aspidistra. Wiping her hands on her apron, she gave my father the same small smile he had seen early that morning—an eternity ago, so it seemed!—and reached into the cupboard for a bottle of beer. Me, I was at the table, gazing at the ceiling; I wanted no contact with my father, none at all, not after last night. He stood in the doorway stamping his boots on the doormat as the fog came swirling round him into the room. He did not return my mother's smile, he did not even attempt the equivocal pursing of the lips he'd managed in the morning. My mother was standing at the kitchen table with her back to him, pouring out a glass of beer. "Close the door, Horace," she said, "the fog's coming in. I've fried you a nice bit of liver—" She was cut short by a loud *bang!* as my father slammed the back door. He stamped across the kitchen floor, frowning, sat down heavily at the table (ignoring me as I was ignoring him) and drank the glass of beer. "Don't drink so fast," murmured my mother, busying herself at the stove. In response to this my father refilled the glass, and in the process the thing frothed over onto the tablecloth, a nice piece of embroidered cambric that had been a wedding present from his late mother-in-law. "Oh Horace," cried my mother, "now see what you've done! Be a little more careful, please." But still her tone was mild, she was determined that they wouldn't fight.

My father didn't care. He was a changed man now, hard as granite and cold as ice. A new sort of anger burned in him, and it burned with a cold, hard, gemlike flame: I could see it in his eyes when he took his glasses off, the hard flame burning in those hard pale-blue eyes of his. He had been a surly, humorless husband and father for years, but never before had I seen in him an anger as fierce, as cold, as this. It was as if he'd crossed a line of some sort, lost the ability to feel even a *spark* of human sympathy toward my mother. The tablecloth, the smiles, the sizzling liver—none of it could touch him, he knew only an urge to push her roughly out of his path, and so strong was the feeling he could barely suppress the violence her very presence aroused in him. He sat at the table without taking off his scarf or his jacket or his boots, without looking at me, without rolling a cigarette, he sat there with a face like tortured thunder and threw back glass after glass of beer until the big quart bottle was almost empty. My poor mother, the effort she was making was immense, and in return she was getting nothing but this wordless fury. "What is it, Horace?" she whispered as she put his plate of liver and onions on the table, pushing aside the houseplant as she did so. "What's the matter with you?" She stood there peering at him with her head slightly to one side and a mass of pained, bewildered wrinkles working on her brow. Nervously she kept wiping her hands on her apron although they were quite dry. My father glared at the steaming liver, his fists to either side of the plate clenched so tight that the knuckles were like billiard balls trapped and straining beneath the skin. "Tell me, Horace," came the voice again, and still he glared, fighting down a wave of sheer black rage, grimly clutching for control, grimly holding on. Get away from me! screamed a voice in his head, but my mother, my poor foolish mother, did not get away, instead she drew closer, reached out a hand, made as if to touch him. At last he turned toward her—the kitchen was silent, for the skillet was no longer sizzling, only the drip of the tap—and what a face he showed her! Never will I forget that face, not for as long as I live: brows knit in agony, lips pulled back from his teeth, all his mouth frozen in a terrible rictus that expressed both violence and utter helplessness, tortured helplessness in the face of that violence, and the eyes!—his eyes were burning not with the hard, gemlike flame now but with the same pain that contorted his brow and his lips, his whole sorry physiognomy, it was all there, and my mother read it and was shocked by the suffering that was in him, and she drew closer. "No!" said my father as her fingers fell upon his shoulder, "No!"—and then, with a strangled sound that half choked him in the utterance he rose clumsily to his feet, knocking the chair over backwards with a clatter, and stumbled across the kitchen to the back door, and out into the fog. My mother stood a moment gazing after him with her fingers pressed to her lips. Then she darted after him, down the yard to where the gate at the end stood open, and into the alley beyond. "Horace!" she cried. But night had fallen, the fog was thicker than ever, and she could see nothing, nor did any sound come back to her through the darkness, and after taking a few steps in one direction, and then in the other, she came back into the yard, back into the kitchen, and closed the door behind her. The chill and stink of the fog could be felt within the room's warmth, and she stood for a moment and hugged herself and shivered. "Oh Spider," she whispered; I was still sitting there, stunned by what had happened. She gazed at the plate of cooling liver and the stain of spilt beer on the tablecloth, and then she sank onto a chair and laid her head on her hands and wept.

o o o

Rain again today. I love rain, did I tell you this already? Also I love fog, and have since I was a boy. I used to love going down to the docks in a fog to listen to the foghorns as they hooted and honked at one another, and watch the pallid glow from the lights of vessels slipping downstream with the tide. It was the cloak of spectral unreality I loved, the cloak it spread over the familiar forms of the world. All was strange in a fog, buildings grew vague, human beings groped and became lost, the landmarks, the compass points, by which they navigated melted into nothingness and the world was transfigured into a country of the blind. But if the sighted became blind, then the blind—and for some odd reason I have always regarded myself as one of the blind—the blind became sighted, and I remember feeling at home in a fog, happily at ease in the murk and gloom that so confused my neighbors. I moved quickly and confidently through fog-blanketed streets, unvisited by the terrors that lurked everywhere in the visible material world; I stayed out as late as I could in a fog. Last night, as I sat scribbling in my garret room at Mrs. Wilkinson's, I got up from time to time to stretch my limbs and gaze down at the rain as it came drifting through the halo of the streetlamp opposite; and realized how little I'd changed, how my emotions in the rain that day (yesterday, I mean) so closely matched the feelings I'd had for fog as a boy. What lies at the root of it all, I wonder, what force is it that once drew a lonely child out into foggy streets and still exerts its attraction in heavy rainfall some twenty years later? What is it about the misting and blurring of the visible world that gave such comfort to the boy I then was, and to the creature I have since become?

Queer thoughts, no? I sighed. I bent down to pull my book out from under the linoleum. Nothing there! I groped. Momentary lurch of horror as I assimilated the possibility of the book's absence. Theft? Of course—by Mrs. bloody Wilkinson, who else! Then there it was, pushed just a bit deeper than I'd expected; no little relief. My father was stumbling blindly through a fog, barely conscious of his whereabouts, the chaos within him further befuddled with the beer he'd just drunk. Great relief in fact; what on earth would I do if she got her hands on it? Is the best place for it really under the linoleum? Isn't there a *hole* somewhere I can tuck it into? The streetlamps were smears of light in the fog, flecks and splinters of weak fractured yellowy radiance that picked up the glitter of wild light in his eyes, the fleeting blur of whiteness of his nose and brow as he charged by. Somewhere I've seen a hole, I know I have, but where, where? On he blundered until at last he saw a building aglow, and like a moth to the flame he drew near, and found himself outside the Dog and Beggar. In he went, into the dry warmth of the place, and suddenly there was the smell of beer and tobacco in his nostrils and the murmur of talk in his ears. I just can't afford to take the chance.

For a few moments he stood there in the doorway, his chest heaving violently as he brought his breathing under control. His eyes were still wild, his skin damp and sleek with the wet. He glanced about the room, with its scattering of small round tables; there was a thin drift of sawdust on the bare wood floor, and standing at the bar was an old man reading the racing results. Two more old men sat at a table near the fireplace, where a small coal fire was burning, their lips working silently over gray toothless gums. All the talk came from the saloon bar, beyond the glass partition, and from that direction Ernie Ratcliff now appeared. Glancing at my father as he laid a thin hand upon a beerpump, he murmured: "Well come in, Horace, if you're coming." And my father, his passions still roiling in his breast, nodded blankly once or twice and closed the door. Like a man in a dream he approached the bar. Ratcliff noticed nothing amiss—or if he did, it was not his way to mention it. "Nasty out," he remarked, "real pea-souper. Pint of the usual, is it, Horace?" My father nodded, and a few seconds later had carried his pint to a table and sat there gazing at the fire.

Then all at once he seemed to awaken, to recognize his surroundings. He picked up his glass of beer and drained almost the entire pint in one draught. He rose to his feet and made his way back to the bar. "Same again?" said Ratcliff amiably. "Nice drop, this" and he pulled my father another pint.

An hour later my father was once more out in the fog. He had not grown calm in the meanwhile, very far from it. The manic turmoil had subsided, but from that subsidence had emerged a decision. Decision, I say; it was more of an impulse, even an instinct, than a decision, a sort of simple blind drive toward the satisfaction of a hunger—and I need hardly tell you what that hunger was. Unsteadily he'd emerged from the Dog and Beggar, buttoned his jacket and tied his scarf about his throat. Then he'd set his steps toward the Earl of Rochester, and been quickly swallowed by the fog, which was thicker than ever.

By the time he reached the Earl of Rochester my father appeared to be under control. He did not lurch, he did not slur his speech, but he was in fact drunk, and no less in the grip of instinct than he had been when he left the Dog. The Rochester was full when he arrived; this was a Friday night, and it was already close to nine. He pushed open the door and stepped quickly inside, a wisp or two of the fog clinging to him as he entered. A wave of chatter and laughter, smoke and warmth and light rolled over him. He pushed his way through to the bar and ordered whisky. When he had it he turned, looking for Hilda.

She was at a table in the corner with Nora and the rest. She glanced up, then promptly rose to her feet and made her way through the crush toward him. Odd, this; you would expect her to make him come to her. I think I know what accounted for her behavior in the Rochester that evening, and for much that occurred afterwards, for I believe she'd learned something about my father since the events in the alley the previous night, something specific; when the time comes I shall explain all this in detail. Now, though, she came pushing through the crowd, her face flushed and a glass of port held aloft in one hand like an ensign, and as she came she bantered with the men, who made way for her, laughing, as a brisk sea parts before a vessel under sail. Then she was beside him, and as he had the first taste of the whisky the bite of the spirit added fuel to the desire he'd been feeling since nightfall. With one boot on the brass rail at the bottom of the bar, and his eyes never leaving her face, he pulled out his tobacco. "So, plumber," said Hilda—she too had been drinking, and she recognized the wildness in him— "feeling better tonight, are we?"

My father was rolling a cigarette, his head lowered and his fingers busy with Rizla paper and Old Holborn, but his eyes were still on her. When it was rolled he lit it with a match and said: "Come down the allotments."

Yes, she could feel how wild he was, and it excited her. "Down the allotments?" she said, lifting her eyebrows and resting her tongue on her top lip. He turned toward the bar, nodded, and drank off the whisky. "When?" she said.

For a few moments he was silent, waiting for the barmaid. He bought himself another whisky, a sweet port for her. They stood among the milling drinkers, and it was as though invisible threads

bound them together. "I'll go now," he said, "you come down in a bit."
Hilda brought her port to her lips. She allowed a small pause
to occur. "All right, plumber," she said, "I don't mind if I do."

I remember where I saw a hole: it's behind the gas fire. It used
to be a fireplace. There's an empty grate and a chimney; that'll do
me nicely, I'll just slip it in there. But I must stop for a minute, all
night I've had the strangest sensation in my intestines, as though
they were being twisted like a length of rubber hosing. Something
odd is going on down there, though just exactly what I don't know;
probably something I ate.

o o o

On I scribbled, on through the hours of darkness, getting
down on paper my exact and detailed reconstruction of that terrible
night, all I'd thought about during those long, empty years cooped
up in Canada. I was in my bedroom when, not long after my father
had stormed out, my mother called up the stairs to me. I came out
onto the landing and there she was, down by the front door in her
coat and headscarf. "I'm going out, Spider," she said, "I shan't be
long." She had put some lipstick on her mouth, I noticed, and a spot
of rouge on each cheek—this was how she looked when she went
out with my father on Saturday nights. It was only Friday, but after
what had happened she could clearly sit no longer in the kitchen.
"I'm going to meet your father," she said, the last words I ever heard
her say in life. I saw her leave the house through the back door, and
I watched her as she stood pulling on her gloves in the yard. She'd
left the light on in the kitchen and for a moment she was bathed in
its glow; this I saw from my bedroom window. Then down the yard
she went, a neat little woman off to meet her husband, and soon she
was swallowed by the fog and lost to my view. But I was *still with
her*, you see, I was still with her as I leaned on my windowsill and
clouded the glass with my breath, I was with her as she moved down
the alley, clutching her handbag, cautiously advancing by the dim
gleam of the lamppost at the end of the alley. She did not know if
my father was in the Dog, nor what sort of reception to expect

should she come upon him there, but she could no longer sit
weeping in the kitchen as he stayed out drinking and seethed with
resentments she did not understand but which apparently, and
through no fault of her own, were directed at her. She reached the
Dog, stepped bravely into the public bar, and walked right up to the
counter. "Evening Mrs. Cleg," said Ernie Ratcliff. "Looking for
your old man? He was here, but I believe he's gone." He peered
about the room with his little weasel eyes. "No," he said, "no sign
of him, Mrs. Cleg."
   "I see," said my mother. "Thank you, Mr. Ratcliff." She was
turning away from the bar when a fresh thought struck her. "Mr.
Ratcliff," she said, "can you tell me where the Earl of Rochester is?"

   I see my father striding through fogbound streets toward the
allotments. Down Spleen Street he strides, the looming gasworks
barely visible above him, along Omdurman Close and across the
bridge over the railway lines, a small dark figure striding through
fog, the ring of his hobnailed boots muffled and dull on the
pavement. When he reaches the top of the path he pauses; the fog
is less dense up here, up on the high ground, and he can just make
out the moon, and off to his left the first of the sheds. He stands there
a moment or two, his figure smudged but distinct against the gray-
black night with its dim blur of moonlight, with the allotments
beneath him and beyond them a maze of streets and alleys falling
away over toward the docks, whence through the fog comes the
mournful hooting of the ships; and a few moments later he is
unlocking the door of his own shed, and then he is in, and fumbling
in his pockets for a match. It is cold and damp in the shed, and in the
darkness, with its strong smell of earth, it is, he thinks, like being
in a coffin. Then the match flares, he lights the candle on the box by
the horsehair armchair, and the flame throws a dull unsteady glow
upon the place. He opens a bottle of beer and paces the floor, his
shadow huge and misshapen in the dim flickering light that the
candle flame casts upon the crude plank walls and raftered gables
of the roof. From out of the shadows of the back wall the eye of the
stuffed ferret suddenly catches the candle flame and casts a sharp
glittering sliver of light across the shed. The alcohol in my father's

system allows him no pause, no peace, in which he might consider what he is doing; he remains in a sort of fever, still driven by that single fixed instinct.

Finally she comes. My father hears her outside and throws open the door. Cursing and stumbling, she picks her way up the path in her bare feet, clutching her shoes in one hand and a bottle of port in the other. "Shit!" she shouts as she sets a foot down in the potato patch. My father is grinning now, and against the dull light spilling from the open shed Hilda sees his white teeth shining as he comes forward to help her. She steps out of the soil back onto the path and he puts an arm around her shoulders; instantly they are cleaving to one another beneath the smoky moon; instantly the heat that has been simmering in my father since nightfall rekindles to a fury as they rock back and forth, pressed close to one another, there on the path outside the shed. Muffled snorts of laughter from Hilda, her face buried in my father's collar, then slowly they come apart, and move toward the shed, then through the door, the door closes, and silence descends once more upon the allotments.

(Dear God I wish silence would descend on this house! They've started up again, and they seem to be *stamping* up there now, they keep it up for minutes on end and then collapse, helpless, apparently, with laughter. I've been standing on my chair and banging on the ceiling with my shoe, but it does no good at all, in fact it only seems to make things worse. Mrs. Wilkinson has much to answer for, and the disturbance of my sleep by these creatures is not the least of it. And my insides still hurt!)

o o o

My mother stood just inside the door of the Earl of Rochester and gazed about her, bewildered. The pub was full, and by this hour a sort of collective madness had infected the patrons so that they talked and laughed and gesticulated like caricatures of men and women, like grotesque puppets, and my mother, meek of heart, and sober, was deeply intimidated. The air was thick with smoke, almost as thick as the fog outside; and in the crush of these people, whose loudness seemed to increase their size while diminishing their humanity, she could get no sort of an idea whether my father was present or not. Meek and sober though she was, she had determined upon a course of action: gripping her handbag she began to push her way through, with frequent mumbled apologies, glancing all about her as she advanced.

At last she reached the bar. She waited patiently for the attention of a barmaid. Whenever one came near, however, some large, florid man would come crowding in from behind her, reaching over her shoulders with huge red fists clutching beermugs and spirit glasses, and begin to recite a long, complicated list of drinks; and the barmaid would be sent scurrying this way and that. This happened several times, and still my mother stood there at the counter, dwarfed by these giant boozers, until at last she won the undivided attention of a friendly young woman who said: "What can I get you, dear?"

"I'm looking for my husband," said my mother. A snort from the man beside her, and a series of uproarious comments from his companions as he repeated her words.

"Who's your husband, dear?" said the harried barmaid, not without sympathy, raising her voice to be heard over the racket.

"Horace Cleg."

"What's that?" said the barmaid.

"Horace Cleg," said my mother.

"Horace!" shouted the man beside her. "You're wanted!" "Is he here?" said my mother, turning to the man. "Not if he's got any sense he's not!" said the man, and they all shouted with laughter.

"Horace Cleg?" said the barmaid. "I don't know him, dear. Regular, is he?"

"No," said my mother. "At least I don't think so."

"Sorry, dear," said the barmaid. "Can I get you something?"

"No thank you," said my mother, and turning away from the bar she pushed back through the crowd to the door, and a moment later found herself out in the fog once more.

She had crossed the bridge over the railway lines and was standing on the path that ran along the allotments; she was staring at my father's shed. The land behind it sloped away steeply, and the gabled roof stood out in sharp definition against the wispy fog and the night sky, in which the moon now seemed more a lump than a globe, like a huge potato. From round the edges of the door seeped a dimly flickering light, so she knew he was in there; what kept her out on the path were the odd muffled noises issuing from the shed; clearly he was not alone.

After several minutes it grew quiet, and my mother, chilled by the night, began to think that she might quite simply walk up the path and knock on the door. But still she didn't move, still she stood there shivering at the gate, staring at the shed and clutching her handbag tight. From the streets beyond the allotments came the desolate barking of a dog, and from the river, the foghorns; then suddenly, behind her, a goods train went steaming by on its way into the city and gave her a start. With no small effort, and no little courage, she opened the gate and walked quickly up the path to the door.

Robert Mapplethorpe Picture

Eileen Myles

Fear of not being understood is the greatest fear I thought, lying on the bathroom floor at 11 PM. Worse than not pleasing people, worse than anything else I can think of. Worse than being cold or alone. Worse than getting old. There used to be a club called the 80s, I announced walking back into the kitchen. Did you know that. Right in the beginning of the 80s when that was a new thing. I went there one night with Yvette. We saw a band, Arthur was in it, that guy we had been shooting junk with, the night I OD'd, I was thirty. Right there with the decade. Yvette's breasts were so lovely and large, her sheets smelled sweet, I loved sleeping with her but Yvette was cruel. She would taunt me for not knowing how to make love to her, though she had pursued me right up to the point of the bed and then I was supposed to perform as the dyke though by all evidence I was undeniably femme. At least with Yvette. But I loved holding her, lying on her couch when we were high. She listened to classical music and the Stones. Some girls. Doo doo doo doo doo-doo, oh I miss you girl. At the 80s we took speed did quaaludes when we got home. Having failed her again in bed I had to get up at 10 to go to Bond Street so I could have my picture taken by Robert Mapplethorpe. Things like this made me welcome in her bed. But I woke up at ¼ of 11. I called and according to Robert Mapplethorpe it was fine. No problem he said. See you at noon. He showed me pictures of Lisa Lyons, incredibly worked out. I looked at pictures of black men, gorgeous men, a penis lying like a turd on a stool. Lisa's fingers lifted, one from each hand—the feminine way to thrust your muscles out. She was big. We smoked a joint, I drank a ginger ale, said no to a beer. I guess we talked about John Giorno who had set this thing up. I said I was a poet. You got a band he said. No. How come he asked. I just write poems. He didn't get it. I felt like I was being lazy. It wasn't true. I worked hard.

You don't know how hard it is to be a lesbian. I think at the time I worked at a hospital taping electrodes to people's jaws and heads so we could watch their dreams. Yvette got me that job, and then she would give me speed so I could stay up and then she mocked me all night because I was a clod. I came to work all nervous with my hair wet in a pink shirt. Thank God I was sexy. I couldn't work with my head. I was always too confused. Robert Mapplethorpe was cute. The kind of boy I really like, slightly evil looking with black curly hair. Motown music played all along. That was how you could tell he was a fag. I mean the shots of the black men could've been about the time which was still loaded with speed and minimalism. Everything was a good idea. A girl with big muscles. We'll try it. Turn your head. Look at me. Look away. Turn your chin. Slightly. Good. Front. Look down. Great. That's it. I'll have prints in about a week. Call me if you want one.

I came back—sorry, "we" did, with Donna, my "real" girlfriend. It was a nightmare, life with her. Finally I had forced her to move out in May but I let her come back in June because I felt sorry for her plus I was broke. Then I met Yvette. At the time I was housesitting for Pat, the art writer who was always trying to make me respectable. Write about art, that's what poets do, he said. Him and his wife would always have me over for drinks. He'd look at his watch, "Company's coming!" He'd look at me. Time to toddle off. If I was an art writer I probably could stay. So Donna was staying in my shack on Third Street. Yvette and me slept in Pat's palacial mansion on St. Mark's Place with framed droppings on the wall from crazy DeKooning's plate. I had not improved in bed, always passed out, but, thanks to Pat, again Yvette was impressed. Donna came to the door one night begging for booze. I passed a bottle of wine out the door—now you promised you'd leave me alone. Who is it Yvette yelled. Just the landlady, I smiled, climbing back into bed to smell her great smell. A pussy too sweet.

Donna went with me to Robert Mapplethorpe's and like I said she was either a monster or an insane lamb. She was wearing a peach coloured V-neck sweater in the middle of the summer. I don't know what she looked like. Robert was coming down the street with

Lisa Lyons and we went up and smoked a joint. He showed me this fabulous picture of me. I looked like a statue—all glowing stone. My eyes look cruel and suspicious. I thanked him for his rendition. I wanted to apologize for bringing Donna—I felt I had blown my opportunity to be whipped and fucked by famous people. I don't know, the occasion was all wrong. I walked home with this woman who was ruining my life, had been doing so for a while.

I come from Boston. My mother has a wall in her home that was reserved for nephews, nieces, grandchildren, happy cookouts, aunts and uncles, my brother, my sister, my step-father, everyone but me. Things didn't last long with Yvette. For example one night I had money so we weren't in the usual situation of her taking me out, paying for my drinks and telling me I was a drunk. She buying the late night pastrami sandwich, paying for the cab, the quaaludes, the coke, everything. But me having money, that was much worse. And I wasn't good at it. Actually I was cheap. We approached some club. Manhattan, a woman's bar and there was a big line so I told the woman at the door I was a reporter for some paper, maybe the *East Village Eye* that I thought I could be writing for. I was writing an article about women's bars in New York. Nice, the tough woman at the door said, returning to a conversation with a friend. You want to wait, I asked Yvette. She nodded no. Walking through Washington Square Park I was crying. I don't know why. She said I was sensitive, and so was my girlfriend and we were both too crazy for her. We were at some party and some woman was flirting with me so I stole her hat and we left and finally I was leaving Yvette's wearing the hat, drinking a beer walking down 9th Avenue crying and I never saw her again.

And that's in ten years. It's nearly the nineties—

I thought of my mother's portrait wall. I had showed Yvette the picture that Robert Mapplethorpe had taken of me. That's why I had a crush on you, she said. That's who you looked like to me. But you're not like that. My mother had this wall in Boston. I went home at the end of that summer, 1980. I said Mom, a famous photographer took this picture of me, why don't you put it on the wall. I don't know if I have a frame to fit it, she said, nervous. Momma you can get one at Woolworth's. Well I suppose you're

right. She sighed. Put it on the teevee for now. I did. And before I
left I wrote on the back in pencil "photo taken by Robert
Mapplethorpe NYC 8/80." This was my favorite kind of art, a dirty
secret. My mother had no idea who Robert Mapplethorpe, Patti
Smith's boyfriend was and no one who ever walked into our house
would know either. Years from now someone would find the
picture of me among the effects of my family and think what a
perverse and egoless writer I was to leave such an important
documentation of my existence in a humble house in Arlington,
Mass. There would be such a future because something would
happen to me. Soon. I was sure of that.

In 1988 I drove to Manchester, Mass. with my girlfriend
Sarah to meet my mother and my sister and spend a weekend with
them. I was determined to find a way to get into her house in
Arlington and get that Robert Mapplethorpe picture off the wall
fast. I needed it. Mom, we were thinking we were going to pass
through Boston so since we've got Sarah's car I was thinking it
would be a good opportunity for me to take that trunk of my stuff
that you're always trying to get me—

"No way." My mother has a way of being emphatic. Of being
inhuman and cold. "Uh, uh, I don't want you in my house when I'm
not there. Who will the neighbors think you are—when they see
New York plates. They don't know who you are. Sorry."

Later I brought this up with my sister who lived in Cambridge.
She was studying massage so Sarah and I were letting her practice
on our bodies. "Of course she wouldn't let you in her house when
she's not there. She doesn't trust *you.*"

My therapist was really great and acknowledged that my
family treats me cruelly. That's probably the reason I got involved
with women like Yvette and later Robin. Luckily Sarah is not like
that at all. Well there was one little thing she said about me at the
table but mostly she's not like that.

Go take it, my mother said the next time I came home and then
she got up and she took it herself right off the wall. Get yourself a
frame, ooh she sighed as she slid the ruthless portrait of me out of
the cheap black frame and underneath my stepbrother and wife and
five kids were sitting on their front porch. It was like discovering

a Rembrandt under an old Norman Rockwell clipped out of the *Post*, something junky like that. Wonderful she said replacing icy me with an entire warm family. I haven't seen that one for quite a while. She sat back down to look at it, smiling.

Sarah says I do look quite a bit younger and points out that my nose was not yet broken and is smaller. Your eyes are glassy. You can tell you were fucked up. I was, I said. I was really fucked up. I was even late—she gives me that look: "You've told me before." Tom says I look much better now. But he always looks at the soul. I could put it in the bathroom. That would be kind of cool. While you're shitting here's a picture of me ten years ago. Robert Mapplethorpe took it. The hair's a mess, did you cut your own hair. Of course. Didn't everyone. Well, all my friends got really good haircuts then. I didn't know you went there. I used to go to the 80s— all the time. It wasn't open long.

Paul says he had the same problem. And him and Robert were very close. File it away he says, getting up to go. That's all you can do. It's been great seeing you, dear.

I tell people how cool he was when he took my picture. How cute he was and how comfortable he made me feel. Oh that must've been before Robert went bad. PCP. Coke. Yep. That was the end of that Robert. He was great.

It's true. My eyes are glassy. Shallow. My hair's dirty too. The jersey was green. Dark green. I had a tan. What kind of frame would make it okay for me to hang it. I could put a vase of white flowers next to it like it was a shrine to the past. You've got to come over and see it sometime. It's kind of scary. I don't understand who she was at all. But that's all right. It's the past.

from *The Break*

Lynne Tillman

The walk to Alice Murphy's apartment is sublime. It's cool this afternoon and perhaps this means that fall is coming sooner than later. I hate thoughts like that. Let fall come when it will. Her house is perched atop a hill, is covered in purple flowers and has a few stone gargoyles shooting out from the roof. Little stones get stuck between my toes as I walk up her path, making my entrance less elegant than I had wanted it to be. This is when I feel old, when in bending down to shake out my shoes, I tremble and need to hold on to the side of the front door. Alice watches this without contempt, I think, and I quickly recover my balance, in all senses.

Paintings and drawings hang on most of the walls, though the room we sit in, a screened-in porch, is underdecorated, bare but for the two chairs and small round table on which is set a pot of tea and small pastries. Three of them, honeyed Greek dainties that eat into the enamel of one's teeth. The view down the hill to the harbor is magnificent and Alice gazes at it with the look of someone who has seen this, and it, all before. She owns the view, not because it's hers—one doesn't own views—but because she has incorporated it into her being. Today she reminds me of Maria Callas, if Callas were an American of Irish and Polish descent. Alice's mother was from the old country and this undoubtedly accounts for her broad jaw, prominent nose and square shoulders. She has always been a good friend to me, though there is a way in which she seems not to need anyone.

Perhaps it is because there is a supreme being for Alice. She believes in God, but I'm not sure what kind of God, and all around her apartment are religious symbols from the major faiths, and probably some of the minor ones too. I can only think, because I think in terms of family and tradition, that Alice must have had an early religious education from which she turned away—it is hard

157

for me to believe her faith wouldn't have been shaken at some time—and to which she returned with renewed fervor after a terrible event. The loss of the child I've already fantasized for her, the acceptance of great failure on her part, the death of a lover, the loss of her singing voice—something must have made her turn again to God. God is a repellent idea to me and were Alice not so spiritually ambiguous in effect, whatever her beliefs, I would not be so fond of her. I would not even take tea with her. But she is and I do, with pleasure.

She pours the tea from a glazed blue teapot as she asks the usual questions. How's the work going? She loves my title, *Household Gods*, for reasons already given, but I'm sure she'd be disappointed or confused by the project were she to read it. No one ever has. The crime/detective stories go out under another name, and no one here reads them, I'm fairly certain—they don't think it's really writing, which bothers me but not so much since I too depreciate their value. I am more than ambivalent about what I produce under the name Norman East. Now I'm not even sure why I chose it. It may have had something to do with East Lynne.

Alice is all in white. White Indian shirt, white duck trousers, which billow about her, white espadrilles. There's a white cotton scarf around her throat and probably she is hiding her neck, which may be crepey, more advanced in years than her face, which is remarkable for its skin's tautness. But the scarf is tied loosely so that she may be wearing it solely for decoration, not to hide her age. Alice doesn't strike one as a woman who would hide anything in an obvious way, simply not to be a cliché, not to appear bourgeois, not to seem to care about what ideally oughtn't be a concern to an intelligent, rational person. But I always think it is the irrational that tells us much more than the rational and I am eager to have her get to the point of our meeting. She does so more quickly than is usual.

"Don't you think it is terrible what young Helen did to poor John Davis?" My first impulse is to say, who is John Davis, but then I vaguely recall seeing from a distance a tall, thin, nondescript guy—I can't think of him as a man—wandering in town about the time Helen arrived; then I saw him no more. Or did I? Dear, what did she do to him, I ask. I have no idea. Alice won't believe this as

I have intentionally laid into my voice a qualified archness, and so she will believe that I know what I don't. I hate not knowing what everyone else knows. She continues, more or less in this fashion: John followed Helen here after she refused to marry him. She led him on. She allowed him to follow her here and now she refuses even to see him. She abandoned him and the poor boy has tried to kill himself. Ah, I retort, you mean that boy. He's not a child, after all, and if she doesn't love him... I'm playing for time. Alice goes on: He's in the hospital and even now she refuses to go to him. And he nearly died. She is horrible to him. It's bad enough that she didn't want his child and had an abortion when he didn't want her to. At this I open my eyes very wide, surely they are popping out. Alice, dear, are you really in a position to blame a young girl just setting out in life for not wanting to be hampered with a child from a man who's wet behind the ears and one she doesn't love? Alice says nothing and looks toward the harbor. And giving up a child for adoption is better? I continue. Now Alice's eyes widen and perhaps it will be this very moment when she can no longer contain within her that horrible secret—the abandoned child, the reckless life she led—but no, she just closes her eyes, takes a breath, during which time she collects herself so as to be able to dissemble, and says, I wouldn't know. I suppose I don't really approve of abortion. Then I say something like, it is a good thing she is living here rather than in the States because she would surely be out of touch with the women who have won the battle for reproductive rights. I feel foolish putting it that way, as if I were making a speech. Perhaps my feminist ancestors are speaking through me, though probably they wouldn't have approved of abortion, either. Come to think of it, it was not always illegal. Still, it is strange to argue what I assume to be the woman's side, with a woman. I would not call myself a feminist, as I am uncomfortable with almost any label, and I am a man, and rather uncomfortable generally with professing to understand the woman's point of view. Yet I don't really believe my being a man ought to keep me from supporting the cause.

Alice and I agree to disagree with some regularity—she has views even more obsolete than my own. Her position in this case demonstrates her stubbornness and a sort of prissy old-fashionedness that may be evidence of her deep secretiveness. Actually I don't believe Alice fully subscribes to what she is saying. I'm sure she's had abortions, as most free-thinking women who have sex lives usually have had. She is being irrational. Perhaps this is serious. John visited me days before he—Alice pauses—he slit his throat. Slit his throat, I repeat, how ghastly. I love the word ghastly. Now I am thinking, there may be more to John, whoever he is, than I imagined. He is a sweet, sweet young man, she says, and I can't see why he clings so to Helen. Alice is calling on me, she has summoned me, to defend Helen, about whom I know not enough, not that much at all. Helen is brilliant, I say quickly, honest, good-natured. She is independent, a different kind of young woman, Alice, very different. She is to me like a new kind of writing I don't quite understand. I say this with a flourish and then sip some tea.

Alice doesn't know what to do with my exaggerated view, my way of putting Helen, and neither do I. It just came to me in a flash, but I think it's true, or rather, I am prepared to defend its truth. Especially if she is my tabula rasa. But then that means I am writing her, and I am not, I don't think, since I couldn't possibly make her up, even though I do try in my way to make it new, as Pound exhorted. It is important to be able to recognize what is new, as I do in Helen. I try, in my real work, to follow that adage. Though on the surface and to the world I myself am not terribly underground in my thinking. Burroughs, for example, is not to my taste. I live my life, in a certain sense, underground, but even that is underground. I don't flaunt anything, except when I'm drunk. There's nothing novel about that. Maybe bohemian or vulgar, but not new. Alice asks me what I'm smiling about. I tell her, as winningly as I can, that I'd once fantasized that Helen was her daughter, that it seemed to me they should like one another. Why don't you? I ask her. What happened when she came here for tea? Nothing, she says, nothing at all. Then, with some hesitation as if biting back more damaging words, Alice admits, she sleeps with too many men, I can't bear it, it upsets me, I feel humiliated for her, and she has no sense to feel shame. The way she walks, she adds. That doesn't, I say primly, sound like nothing. Perhaps she is guileless, I add, rather than shameless. But why then have you offered her piano lessons? Alice says she is older than Helen and ought to set an example, especially as she hasn't had children, nor did she ever want them. I suppose I feel guilty, Alice adds with reluctance. Ah, guilt, I repeat, I am no stranger to that. I smile at her fondly. I do wonder who she's involved with now, if she is. She's more secretive than I, surely.

Alice walks down the hill with me. She is going to visit John in the hospital. Just before we left her house she applied a peachy lipstick to her full mouth and now looks herself, overall, rather peachy, reminding me of Renoir's still-life of that fruit. There's some excitement in her gait. She may be in love with John. Why not? I like young men too. Perhaps, she says to me as we go our separate ways—quaint but true—perhaps I am being harsh. But suicide, Horace, and he's very special. We cluck each other on the cheeks like two ageing hens.

Alice disappears in white down the dusty road. I feel full and weightless. It's mad but I enjoy the melodrama enormously and suddenly feel that I am privy to Helen's life, the one she hides from me. Perhaps she doesn't hide it. Simply doesn't mention it. After all, that was the vow I took with her—not to ask, not to pry, to be free of all that.

The hotel is divided, cast equally in sun and shade, appropriately enough, I reflect. Nectaria greets me—Yannis, Horace—and I greet her and take the mail. Where is Yannis? There Helen is on her deck—she says Greece is like southern California. I've never been. Her head is down; she is reading a book, and just now she looks behind her and I see a form in the doorway to the terrace, a male form. It looks like Yannis from here, but that's mad. Besides the figure is taller, like John though that too is mad as John is in the hospital. And when Yannis appears here moments later I am assured that I am crazy, driven by paranoia, the fate of homosexuals, wrote Freud, driven to bizarre conjurings and hallucinations, to flee the face of the true loved one. Alice could be right about Helen, of course, it is within the realm of possibility. Helen might be cruel, sadistic in the extreme. Amoral. But it is not probable. I am not paranoid about her. In any case I don't subscribe to Freud's theory about paranoia. Doubt is doubt, as a cigar is just a good smoke. Helen waves to me suddenly, just when I'd forgotten I was looking at her. And she makes circles around her eyes with her fingers. A movie tonight? Why not?

Why not? Because I ought to be working, finishing my detective/crime story. A rich boy murders his mother and father, a story based on a case that occurred not far from where I grew up. I knew boys like him. I might have been a boy like him, if I'd been richer and more aggressive, even more twisted than I am. The rich boy evades the law—has an alibi—until a canny, sarcastic private detective, Stan Green, discovers some evidence that the boy thought he'd done away with. But he hadn't, otherwise there'd be no story. I'm nearly at the end of it, but am lately filled with such ennui, I wonder why go on, why bother—and my novel *Household Gods* awaits, petulantly, in a special box, one I've had since college, with a drawing of a rat in the style of Michaelangelo on its cover. A cloud shoots across the sun and covers it; the sky darkens and with it my mood. Just like that, just as if I were a Manichee or some such dualist. Why does one have to do anything, especially if one is, as I am, relatively well-off, especially here. Might I not just while away my short time on this mundane stage rather than engage in the drama of creation? Blow it out your asshole! Roger's crude phrase echoes heartlessly. I laugh aloud anyway. Yannis glances at me skeptically. Roger's right occasionally, right on the money, as they say, even if he doesn't have any money, another one of those things that makes our friendship tense.

It's 5:30 pm, and where has time gone; the day is gone. I must have been with Alice for an hour and have been sitting here for an hour or more, staring into space and toward the harbor and then inwardly, inward staring, navel gazing, my father called it. There is a word for that, Greek, of course, which has come into English: omphaloskepsis, or meditating while staring at one's navel. Marvelous, isn't it. I love words. I shuffle across the floor, slap aftershave on my puffy face, ask Yannis whether he wants to join us, and leave without him, running, not exactly, to the spot where Helen and I always meet.

She is punctual, which I find disarming in a young person. She is even waiting for me, sitting on the curb and reading a book. As I approach she closes it and pats it, as if saying goodbye or, more likely, adieu. She takes my arm and without a word, except Hello, we walk toward the outdoor cinema to see an old Clint Eastwood movie. *The Good, The Bad and The Ugly*—it's been here many times before, but it's always such a pleasure. I'm very glad the Italians took up the Western when we'd let it drop, which was as it should be, given the history it covered over or distorted. But still, and I hate to admit it, I love those early Westerns and the picturing of the bold and brave crossing the old frontier. I can feel my breath nearly stop when all the wagons line up next to each other, or behind each other, ready for the shout—Westward Ho!—that starts the dangerous journey. And I know all of this is wrong to feel—there is such juvenile pride in these feelings—and the West couldn't possibly have looked the way it did in the movies; and Turner's thesis was incorrect anyway. But, for a movie, it's breathtaking—the screen filled with women in bonnets and men in rawhide. I suppose rawhide smells horribly. The Italians don't go in much for wagons in circles. But those close ups! Clint Eastwood is not my type at all, though I like his squinting in the sun and chewing on a stogie. The lines at the corners of his eyes are deep as burrows in the ground and I think of Alice Murphy and the thin, scratchy lines about her eyes, her pale pale eyes. Helen's knees are clasped to her chest, she's like a human ball curled up into herself. Of course mental patients do that too, and rock back and forth. Perhaps her uterus hurts her. Oh hush, Horace, I say to myself. Shut up. The movie's so exaggerated, the actors, their gestures and expressions, the delineation between the good and the bad, and the music so wonderful that after a while I do forget the lines around Alice's eyes and the questions about Helen and John. It's a long movie, time will stretch and stretch here. I feel happy. I take Helen's hand and squeeze it and she looks at me furtively and I realize she's crying. Tears are most definitely in her eyes, but could they be there for any of the characters on the screen? It seems unlikely. I hand her my handkerchief and she takes it with a small laugh, so she must be all right. Nevertheless she does wipe her eyes and, I might add, blow her nose. It's possible she's allergic to the weeds or something in the air.

The Greeks are swinging their worry beads full force now. I

tried them when I was first here but discovered that I am in no way the sort to be able to go native. I felt completely ridiculous. Helen is not the type, either, which relieves me. As we walk out of the theater several men make quite a show of watching her bottom— her ass—and I pretend not to notice them. But Helen turns on her heel and in Greek tells them to fuck off. They are as astonished as I am. My Smitty, my Helen, is full of surprises. She has yet to disappoint me in any important way and if she's now being crude, it is her right, for, I ask myself, why should she let those men devour her with their greedy eyes and make rude comments. Still the speed and harshness of her attack is a shock. Helen takes my arm and we walk back to the harbor.

These are the only Westerns she likes, she tells me, she can't sit through the others. A twinge of sadness and even futility at this gap between us settles just below my breastbone or in my solar plexus where sadness resides, I think. Certainly I can't adequately explain to her my sense of loss, my nostalgia for the U.S. ones, mendacious as they are. She'd be out of sympathy with me, though I'm sure she'd listen attentively and without malice. Helen doesn't make fun of me. Were I to express myself she'd respect my opinion and be very interested, intrigued at how differently I thought from her. Still I'm embarrassed, mentally enfeebled, as if hobbled for a moment by age; I am determined not to let that show. Jovially, and with a little bow, I invite her to dinner. But no, she won't join me. And no, I can't find the words to ask her about John and besides I'm not supposed to. She says she is going to see the Gypsy woman the next day. But will she visit John, I wonder, and don't dare ask.

I might visit John. I just might. Suddenly that comes into mind—rather than having to ask Helen anything. She might not like my doing it but I'm free, as is she. I could pay him a call in the hospital—do a good deed, be a good Samaritan. Tell him Alice said he wanted company. She didn't say he didn't. Alice never mentioned the idea at all. John could be entirely harmless or a malevolent liar and it would be perfectly within reason for me to want to see if what Alice thinks is true or has any relation to reality. Even a trace. Since Helen is my good friend.

The water dashes against the harbor, excited by something

stirring beneath it. A beast, a hideous octopus is moving down below, a war between monsters of the deep, that kind of thing. The restaurant beckons and I take my usual table. The wine is cold and tingles in my gullet and on my tongue. Alice is not here tonight, which is good, as I might feel compelled to reveal something I oughtn't, but that awful Wallace is. Is he out of jail so soon? Do I have to talk with him? He's not really one of our crowd, such as it is, but an interloper on the scene, a madman, different from Stephen whom I haven't seen in months. Perhaps Wallace will tell me again his idea for irrigating the Sahara—some gigantic tube that sucks water from a fertile source, carries it miles and expels it into the parched desert. And he tells his idea with such unwarranted excitement he means it to be taken seriously.

Wallace plops down at my table, uninvited, pulling along his Dutch girlfriend who understands his Afrikaans. I ought to feel pity for Wallace, in and out of mental asylums and jails, this last time for indecent exposure, which could have gotten him kicked out of the country, but someone—probably Roger, he plays chess with one of the judges—interceded. And because Wallace's parents own one of the newspapers in South Africa, and all that was trotted out—his respected books of poetry along with his mother and father whom Wallace despises, their politics and so on—he was set free. And here he is. I wish I'd been on the beach last week when he ran into the water wearing a red net bikini bathing suit. Not the thing to do here, even if men expose themselves, and certainly touch themselves, regularly. They do it furtively—but not Wallace, he's a flaunter. I ought to have sympathy for him—committed to a mental institution when he was just a boy of sixteen, deemed insane for opposing apartheid. He was sane then but has over the years lost whatever marbles he had, I think, though occasionally he's lucid and amusing. I find it hard to tolerate him. He talks so much, in that irritating accent.

I cut my fish, lifting the flesh away from the bone. My hand is steady and as usual I wonder if I oughtn't to have become a surgeon since I enjoy doing this so much. I always think this when I cut flesh, exactly the same thought, and always wonder, in precisely the same way, if others have the same exact thought when they do simple tasks over and again, and then what would it be like, if that were so, to be working in a factory, on the line, doing the same job daily, repetitively? I do a good job with my fish and feel satisfied. Little things please me. My mother could never serve fish that was not riven with bones. I hated fish, the way most children do, and it took me years to develop a taste for it, and if I hadn't I couldn't have made my home in Greece.

At the moment I seem to be invisible at my own table, which is to my liking. Wallace and his friend chatter away in Afrikaans. I'm sure his Dutch girlfriend is a kind soul but I have an antipathy to the Dutch and may be the only non-Belgian or non-German so inclined, or disinclined. Years ago I visited Amsterdam and had a most dreadful time. I stayed a few months, it rained constantly, and I met no one and found the Dutch barely civil. Everyone says they're so nice, so I never interject that I think they are dull. Actually I don't know if they are but I nurse my secret dislike, my prejudice, and allow it to develop unhindered by scrutiny. The Dutch, I want to tell Wallace, have given tolerance a bad name.

I don't know how Wallace held up in court or if he had to face the judge at all. What does his girlfriend find appealing about him? This is a man who is never at a loss for the ladies, to be euphemistic about it. He's had more lovers than one would ever guess from looking at him; only something like a distorted notion of sexual freedom could have allowed this outrage, this flourishing of a lunatic Don Juan. Wallace professes to adore the female sex and has set many poems in bedrooms where his beloved lies *deshabillée* on a bed, which allows him to describe in fanatic detail the beauty of the female body, the pearl he nuzzles with his nose and licks with his tongue, that sort of thing. But what do they see in him? Maybe when he was young he had a certain *je ne sais quoi*...But now? Paunchy and dishevelled. He has the worst set of caps I've ever seen. He whistles through them when he speaks. His eyes protrude like mine. And he tends to leer when he looks, a mad intensity; I suppose someone else might say it signalled genius but to me it is most hilarious, signifying nothing like intelligence. The girlfriend's not laughing. Where the hell is Roger? Oh dear, Wallace is reading his poetry out loud, in English, something about a dog. I'm barely listening. Roger might relieve me of the burden of seeming to listen to Wallace. I know Roger plans to get money off Wallace, for some scheme or other, to buy property here through a Greek lawyer, to open a cafe. Roger always has something on the boil; he's one of those kinds of people who keeps things moving by concocting ideas—for money, usually—that other people ought to invest in or become involved with. A magazine he'd run or a property he'd administer. Sometimes they do give him money, but I never have. It's a point of pride with me.

Wallace has stopped reciting his poem. Now he's defending Pound to the Dutchwoman. She must be completely uninterested. He's whistling on about T.S. Eliot, being fierce as usual about Pound. He says it's because he, Wallace, and Pound are both traitors but I think it's that Pound's support of Fascism was a kind of temporary psychosis. Wallace is more paranoid than I could ever be and he is rabidly heterosexual. Though, again, I can't see why any woman would want to sleep with him. I've often noticed that even the most unpleasant men attract reasonable and kind women and these women put up with these men for ages. They cook and clean for them, tidy up their social messes. And what for? The love of genius. It's not likely that genius could be attached to so many miscreants. Sometimes the women are masochistic, but then so am I, I should think, in some ways, and I'd never want a man like Wallace. He's unbearable. He seems to think he was in St. Elizabeth's with Pound, insisting that he did visit him and even hid behind a tree to watch him after he was supposed to have left the hospital grounds. I hope he was sane when he did so, although it doesn't sound as if he was. Just imagine how Pound must have felt to be incarcerated, surrounded by manic depressives and schizophrenics, and then have an ambulatory lunatic pop up, raving as wildly as any in there with him. I don't believe Pound was truly insane. In this I agree with Wallace. He got caught up in temporary mayhem and played possum, as Wallace now declares. Wallace has dropped to the ground to imitate a possum, and his girlfriend is urging him to stand up or sit down. This is tiresome.

I look away. Helen is on her terrace. The sun has almost entirely set, leaving behind glorious slashes of red and purple in the darkening sky, streaks of color like the streaks of blond in her thick brown hair. She's turned one light on and it's hanging above her head but she's not reading. Drawn to the light as I am, Wallace gazes at Helen and says that he met "that young woman"—he knows her name—at the market and asked her if she ever intended to marry and would she consider him if she was. Wallace says that he dropped to one knee to ask her for her hand and that Helen laughed and told him to get up. His girlfriend is not pleased. What is her name? Something guttural—Brechyah or Gretchya. Wallace insists that he asked her to marry him simply to make her feel better for surely a woman on her own is lonely. The life of a spinster is barren, he told her. I can just see Wallace doing that and imagine Helen's disgust. He seems to have a penchant for dropping to the ground.

Once, when he was in Paris, Wallace trotted about the city wearing a pith helmet and dunked his head under the cascading waters of various stone fountains. He filled his pith helmet with water to throw over himself. It was a hot summer. He showered in the street and lay on the ground next to Notre Dame until the gendarmes removed him. That was the summer his mother came to Paris to see him, to rescue him from the Beats and so forth. But Wallace was not for rescuing. He enjoyed the bohemian life and also enjoyed throwing himself at his mother's feet, accusing her in a loud moan of driving him crazy. When he tells this story he always notes, my mother shook and so did her gold jewelry. He loves making a scene.

Roger is approaching, affecting his usual manly gait and I spy a peculiar little smirk on his lips that I'd like to rub off. Or rub out, rub him out. I must be drunk or Helen is right and I hate him. He kisses the Dutchwoman's hand elaborately and Wallace sits up, like a well-trained dog, to pay attention to him, as if to a teacher. Roger to my eye is in no way commanding. He can be pedantic, though. They all chatter together aimlessly for a bit and Roger asks how my book is going and if I didn't finish a big chunk the other night. My work is progressing, I lie, and yours, dear? I'm past the hurdle, he says, as if I believed him. Then he goes on to talk about his novel, its structure, as if all we wanted to hear about were his artistic trials and accomplishments. It is one thing to discuss a literary subject, it is quite another to complain endlessly about the difficulty of writing. These things, I believe, ought never be the subject of discussion. Would a carpenter take up the dinner hour telling all assembled how hard it was to finish this or that job? No, he'd get on with it. And if he were intelligent he might talk about an aspect of carpentry about which all assembled might learn something. Carpentry affords many metaphors. You're airing your laundry, I say to him. In this you and I have no meeting of the mind. Unhappy with my castoff, he answers, pointing at Yannis who's nearly moribund, suffering from boredom at another table. Oh Roger, I retort, in mock horror, you are *trés* transparent. And you, Horace, he answers, are in no position to judge. Yannis, I assume, has heard Roger's remark and this bodes ill for the rest of the evening.

The evening ends as most do. It blurs into a watery mass of colors, amorphous moments and words, the night's palette. Not the bed. Helen's light is out. I wonder if she is making love. I want to make love though that is not what Yannis and I often do. He sometimes permits me to love him and occasionally he responds or services me. I content myself with the past. There was a love of my life, years and years ago. He and I shared a bed and a home for fifteen years, and it ended finally and suddenly, broken off mysteriously and mutually after a petty quarrel, and I've never understood it, and that was twenty years ago, and he's been dead for ten, and I never again lived with anyone, not after him. I was involved with a few, but none like him.

Yannis is no grand passion, not even a small one. He's a comfort to me, and sometimes is not, as when I am irritable from drink and he is sulking about some inflicted wound. I have a sharp tongue and say things I don't mean, most of which I'm sure he doesn't understand, but the boy has a terrific capacity for dark moods, which sometimes frighten me. I try to cheer him up with gifts and small trips. I don't understand him and he certainly doesn't understand me. He thinks I just type, for example, and I think—I don't know what I think. I am too old to expect more. I am ridiculous. My body is decaying, the flesh literally weakens and drops from the bone, gravity is pulling at my skin, I grow old, I grow old. Alice says it's the drink and perhaps she is right.

T.S. Eliot understood decay. I've often said that was his métier. But need and lust, for me that has not changed, not for me, though my body weakens, melts, grows tired and loses its hold, its grip on life. It doesn't matter and more's the pity, because my thoughts are the same, and if I allow myself to have these primitive, primordial, ageless feelings, they make me young again, in my mind, and I feel a blast of lust, of full-bodied, young desire rising up from my darkest self. Then it rushes furiously into my mouth and to my genitals and settles there, and gets cold and solid and still, and I can taste it, like Proust's madeleine. I can become terribly sad, despondent, wanting to rage against this inevitable fate, rage like so many men before me. Sometimes I want to die.

I often picture my funeral, even when I'm happy, especially when I'm happy. I see the faces of friends, back in the States where I'll be buried, of course, in the family plot, just beneath, in the row below, that is, my father and mother. My parents visited their future gravesite once a year, to place flowers on their mothers' graves— their mothers knew each other well as they were first cousins—and I was taken along, my spot pointed out to me with pride. At my funeral—I can see it very clearly—friends who haven't heard from me for years and years will come and remember me in prep school and college, then my publisher will say a few words, and some of the New York crowd, whoever's alive, will make the trip, and say how charming I could be, and so forth. I will leave the world in relative anonymity. It's unbearable to me. I drink until I can drink no more.

The black sky is bottomless, fathomless like death and life too, and it comforts me in a way Yannis can't, which is not the dear boy's fault. He's fallen asleep on the bed, a body made tender by unconsciousness. I am looking out at the harbor, still as death at this time of night. Nothing is moving but the water and the clouds. Even the wind blows silently. The air is cold and startling. The night gods have chilly breath. Whatever paradise is, it must happen when everyone's asleep, when there can be no complaints, and that must be why night gets so dark, so that we cannot see any imperfections in our world and so there can be nothing to complain about. Pound tried to write paradise at the end. He wrote: Let the wind speak, that is paradise. My enduring, stubborn passion must be written on the wind. And there it goes, there it goes, blown away by an indifferent blast of silent night air. Helen's light is finally out.

Laüstic

Wendy Walker

When her husband's step had faded on the stairs, Thessala looked down at the blood on her gown. The small red bursts on her chest were irregular; one straggled wetly towards a lower star. The feathered body still flowered in the stain of her lap, its creamy throat blameless of color, its wings arching from breathless sides. Of what remained, only the legs, spreading impossibly, betrayed an unnatural flight. She scanned the floor for the other part, that had uttered for her so many nights. The black bead, upside-down, returned her blank look from the boards; with just such an intentness the little head would have stared had Raindurant allowed her the creature. So thinking, Thessala began again to feel. Her body kept listening: to perfidious echoes of nets in the wind; to her own soundless raving; to the black lake welling in her heart. Fed by underground sluices, their valves shut till he chose to throw them, its darkness was drowning her whole sea. Her hands fluttered. She rose, retrieved the nightingale's head, and placed the dismembered body near the sill. Before she could understand anything, she had to put this gown away. She undressed, sponged herself, and got into a shift and robe. Then she rummaged in the chest for cloth, some white samite, its border stitched in gold. Tenderly wrapping the bird in the bloody gown, she turned her chair from the window, from the garden, the sky, the sight of the neighboring house. She reached for the samite and sat. The afternoon light now fell full on her lap. She opened the box in which she kept spools and needles, and threaded the thinnest with fine black silk floss. Putting Raindurant from her, and fastening Guivret's shape close, she set the point to the top left-hand corner, and began to make pictures with thread.

o o o

Thessala is sitting at her window the first time she sees him. He wanders out into the garden on his side. Putting his hands on his hips, he surveys his new property; then, as though feeling her eyes, he looks up, catches her there. Hesitating, he decides to make no salute; she quickly withdraws. When she returns minutes later, the garden is deserted.

Thereafter she hears him much spoken of. Her husband mentions him first: "Our new neighbor is a very reputable man. You did not grow up here, and probably don't realize that the Kerbols are the oldest family in Saint Malo. It shows great enterprise that such a man should choose to reside in our quarter. I wager, Thessala, that it will not do my business any harm to have such a scion right next door."

It is not long before even her own servants are discussing how good Sir Guivret is: how even-handed and generous. These qualities stand that much higher in relief when she views him in her husband's company. The caution so readable in Raindurant's smooth manner renders his neighbor's lack of guile the more winning. Indeed Thessala comes to find the greatest pleasure in watching the two men together. Her husband's dross makes her neighbor's lights sparkle; Raindurant sets off Guivret like a jewel. These occasions, however, form only the earliest scenes of her joy; for what could compare with those moments in which she grows certain Guivret is in love with her? She cannot miss how her presence shocks him; it happens more than once. It is as though the sight of her makes the ground gape beneath his feet; he tries at first to dissemble these moments, but later takes care that his politeness bear an emphasis she cannot escape.

If she soberly regards these instances, and refuses to look out of her window for a week of dry days, she can with a modicum of discipline damp down her certain joy. Then she will sleep the night through, heavily, matching Raindurant's oblivion with a vintage of her own. But at length, the window seduces her; she cannot deny it much longer than the need of her eyes. The hunger inside her head can only be slaked, it seems, by the window: she wi!l sit, studying the garden wall and bisected turf for whole afternoons.

It is during these sessions that Thessala herself falls in love. As she relives each moment, its full flavor yields to her; comprehending, she topples. Her ravishment is thus constructed and strengthened during the long hours. Her lover's first overtures, received by her only in retrospect, are more forcible now than when made. Near him, she is too stunned, or too rapt; she grasps what has passed when alone.

So Thessala learns that silent language the discreet call Love. She understands how apprenticed she has been to this task through the years. She looks with new eyes on the care she has taken to choose and match finery. Guivret's appreciation, his fathomless comprehension of what she hopes and strives, by minute adjustments, finally to intend, confers a legitimacy marriage has not. His eyes spell assemblage of meaning; the proffered is what he accepts. If she has studied honest science of costume, of style, of enhancement, if she has poured hours into fittings and paint-pots and mirrors, it is in pursuit of a vivid legend. Guivret's way of taking her, to which his sensual shock testifies, repays those alchemical days. She has learned to speak without speaking; has not lost the straightly guarded hours. Her powder's pallor, the tint of her rouge, the coil of her hair and her several brocades, legibly cancel the precedence of privilege; no one can say, from the way she appears, where she was born, who her father was. To work for this can seem little; but to achieve it! At the same time she cannot but wonder at the man who, scanning her lines, fully trains himself on her person.

So Thessala and Guivret continue to give and take words, in silence, in writing, aloud. The closeness of the two houses aids this. Side by side, from the hall to the rooftops, they inevitably study each other. From various windows one may glance at smiles across the way; but from one pair it is possible to converse softly, or throw small packets back and forth. At first Thessala loses all speech at Guivret's subtle daring. The discretion for which she is grateful combines with a ravishing boldness that shakes all her fear into flame. When he sends her a token by her husband, when he tosses a note while the kitchen wench plucks herbs below, she can feel her entire life stop: the breath goes; then her body rebounds from its stammer. She catches the note, comments upon the mannerly present. But did Guivret not measure their chances accurately, she would resent it. Did he ever fail in exercise of care, she would quite keep her feet. But his ways of loving are a poetry; all his deathly risks flourish success; they discover such unforeseen form, the two lovers inhabit a place no one else thinks of noticing. It subsists in Saint Malo, unperceived. As the neighbors lean out of their windows, as they feast, and fashion tender words, the half-timbered heaps quite dissolve. Their very speech makes bodies out of houses, turns casements to eyes.

Thessala will always remember the days of their love: the ambush of sweet immobility, desire soothed by its own return. They find nothing imperfect except the limit of their pleasures. Each treads ethereally, satisfied and glad, a stillness pitted with bright hungers. These cravings, instant and desperate, tunnel the cold ground into spring. When Raindurant leaves Saint Malo on business, commending his wife to strict watch, Guivret feels he can hardly bear it. To have Thessala so close he can see the moisture on her neck, and yet not be able to hold her! In the starriest cold hours, when the two households are fast asleep, the lovers sit in their windows and whisper. Guivret hallucinates touching thorough as moonlight's; Thessala finds rest in frank draughts of his face. She feeds on his eloquence, hoarding it for later surfeit; he drinks in the lustre that bathes the edged slopes of her skin.

It continues this way through the tumble of leaves into snow. By midwinter, though no word of struggle is uttered, the tones of their silence have changed. They read in gesture, in pause, the fateful evolution of quietude. As their certainty waxes, they speak the more with less and less. Love grows invisible as it enlarges; can this continue? Thessala shuns ecstatic doubt. She keeps sentences at a distance. She turns Guivret's notes, even his heady text, into shapes. Guivret, watching her, passes out of his shining elation; or learns the art of hiding. He quashes his body's proud speech. His adoration modulates into loving discernment; he sees what her love for him means. And the excessive room of his happiness welcomes sad safeguards, limits, decrees. As he practices a more restrained wooing, Thessala feels her passion quicken. His recoil exposes a broad field where trust can cavort.

But all that autumn she watches the ivied wall shiver and molt. Its wasting reveals stones whose harsh, unmatched edges float as such sharp things never do. All winter, as she stares, they obtrude through the long brittle branches. Their blotched skin shows freckles of white.

Her gratitude makes arid landscapes fertile; but why shake one's hair in the wind? She seeks weather for sudden spaciousness; she awaits giant furnishings. No stormy cabinet supplies her. Guivret's tact makes Thessala survey distances as she has never done before: how wide, how tall, how far away? She attends to the smallest measures. On her pilgrimage to Morieux she emulates all she sees. Her body performs secret gestures. She takes the postures of pinnacles, the long stretch of receding tides. Borrowing crazy balance from boulders, copying, she collects enough peculiar habits to populate her solitude. Like gowns stiff with riches, they await her need. Branches' jagged meander, the green hair that drips by the sea, the languor assumed by dead fish, all become Thessala. The months pass until she is Brittany. She leaves Morieux, returns home. The wall burgeons; she is ready for that lace. Feeling certain her close observation abets the new buds, she watches each tendril's unfolding. When the air simmers with fragile wings, the wall has entirely succumbed. Its shaggy coat surges and breathes. That the sea, in disguise, should so infiltrate the city's heart makes Thessala's love seem more possible. She receives new hope about stones; she meets her husband's eyes completely.

Everywhere she looks the world seems to be uttering. The green blush, birdsong thick as bushes, the orchard's white bursts, press upon her. Imitating these, Thessala plummets. And in that exulting wordlessness she finds her own love. Emerging, she speaks with a difference: her sentences live in two worlds.

More and more often the night finds her sleepless. She waits for her husband's breathing, then slips from the sheets. She cannot deny herself. She leans out the window. There he is, in a casement below. He hovers, blue in bluer dark; she makes a like shape for him. Guivret feels its sorrow. She reads his intense lingering. She wants to publish her desire to the night. But joy battles fear for dominion over her sentences. Her feeling for truth contends against the breathing nearby. Both summon arabesques of knowledge. So she broods in the guises of things. If she could only be things, not Thessala, she could have innocence and love; moreover, things don't shrink from murder. For things, the world is always whole.

Then one night while she keeps her vigil, Raindurant's voice breaches her thought.

"Why do you rise so often, Thessala? You never sleep when I'm in bed."

Though the question surprises her, she does not start. She amazes herself by how blithely she answers, "Do I really rise that often, Raindurant?" She sighs back at his silence, and turns again to the window. She seizes upon the first thing that strikes.

"Listen! Can you hear it? It's the nightingale! We've never had one in the garden before. How its voice dissolves the night! It expresses everything! It is to listen, husband, that I sit here, awake, in sad hope of clues as to saying; and for the joy of it! This bird takes hearing beyond music, beyond reason, beyond all reproach and appeal! Who has ever heard such a singing? What viol could so stir the heart?"

Raindurant hesitates in the darkness. She feels him considering. He makes his displeasure precise.

"Come back to bed now, Thessala. I want you in bed, beside me."

The next day she watches the gardener lime the whole garth. He smears the lower branches completely, and laces the treetops with mesh. Each afternoon he disappears in the foliage and emerges with tangled birds. He puts them in a cage built for rabbits. Then he reclimbs the ladder, with fresh snares draped over his shoulder.

One day while dreaming, she hears her husband chuckle as he strides up the stairs. When the door opens, she sees his smile. The bird in his hands is struggling.

Here, Thessala, here he is, limed and taken! It has troubled me, how you don't sleep. Be easy, for now you will rest! This little fool won't disturb you again."

She is near him before she knows what to do. The pulse inside his fingers sets her own. Her husband has not, for some years, been more close to her. Measuring the moment, she sinks to her knees.

"Oh, Raindurant, let me keep him!"

He looks down: a flower unfolded, outspread. Such transfiguration would not enrage if he could see his own shape. When she finds his eyes, he meets such boundlessness there, he cannot answer it. An unrest flows to his hands.

"Give him to me, Raindurant, I beg you!"

His merriment turns to woe. Thessala draws hope from his speechlessness. But the reply takes a form. She watches him fold the bird so close it grows still; his wrists, parting, begin to twist. The feathered clump bursts as it's torn. His grimace is blocked out by furious, stained, hurling hands. She feels blows, as of small fists; red scumbling appears on her breast. As the parts simply fall, she heeds his departure: a roar inchoate as an ecstasy; then his clattering step on the stair.

Thessala gathers the small body up as she weeps. Its modest plumage, still warm, has availed it nothing. Raindurant, his gardener, the net-weavers, cage-builders, toss and die in her ruthless seas. As the floods exult in possessing, hatred for sentences, for all laws and all risks that fail, for loss that promises salvation, such hatreds lay claim to her heart.

"How can this be?" she cries. "I cannot rise anymore, not for you, not for him, not for anything! You'll not sing, and he'll think I've forgotten!"

At last she exhausts her tears; she sets the poor creature aside. She opens a chest and takes from it an ivory cloth, folded. For a moment she broods on its blankness. Then she threads a silver needle. The blood on her gown is quite dry. As she coaxes pictures from the samite with her wooing point, she regains a cool, desirous daring. When she has shown all she knows in a brightly clotted web of figurings, Thessala breathes deep; then she knots the last stitch of her gift.

o o o

When Guivret admitted the servant from the house next door, he knew at once something had happened. He received the soft bundle and carried it upstairs. There, alone, he unwrapped the dead bird and studied Thessala's embroidery. He wept. The thought of vengeance occurred to him without making sense. He rejected such an easy course. He went to the window and looked out. Thessala of course was not there. The gardener was removing the nets from the trees. In the days that followed Guivret sold everything he owned. With the money gained he purchased gems. Rubies, coral, carbuncles and pearls, only those both lustrous and rare would he accept. He commissioned a golden coffer, to be embellished with these stones. He specified its dimensions and required strong clasps fitted on each side. When the coffer was ready, Guivret laid the nightingale inside it, shrouded in Thessala's samite. He had the box sealed. He went abroad, carrying it, even though it might attract thieves.

Although Guivret never gave his reasons, and Thessala thereafter silently kept her husband's house, their adventure could not be hidden. Throughout the country it was chewed endlessly, avidly. At length the Bretons made a lai, which they called the Nightingale's: the *Laüstic*, in their own tongue. Marie made a poem of it; a scholar englished it; that is how it came to me.

ABOUT THE AUTHORS

PAMELA BALL is the recipient of a Florida Arts Council Grant for fiction and the 1990 winner of the Hemingway Award for the short story competition. Her fiction has appeared in various periodicals and she is at work on several novels. She lives and works in Tallahassee, Florida.

OWEN GOODWYNE was born in Jacksonville, Florida, in 1947. He has been working on a long, on-going novel for the past several years. He is an attorney half-time and writes the remainder. He has lived in Tallahassee, Florida, since 1970.

BARRY HANDBERG is a novelist who lives and works in Gainesville, Florida.

ED MARSICANO has been writing for twenty years. He published his first short story in *The Apallachee Quarterly* in 1979. In the eighties, he wrote forty short stories, a book of non-fiction and two novels. He also taught cultural history at Bainbridge College for twenty years. He travels in the summers, and lives in Havana, Florida.

BOB SHACOCHIS won the 1985 American Book Award for *Easy in the Islands,* his first collection of stories. Among his many other honors and awards are the American Academy of Arts and Letters Rome Prize, a James Michener Award, a grant from the National Endowment for the Arts, and *Playboy's* Best First Fiction Award. His journalism appears frequently in *Harpers Magazine,* where he is a contributing editor. He is also the author of a second collection of stories, *The Next New World,* and is currently at work on a novel set in Virginia and the Caribbean. He lives and works in Tallahassee, Florida.

GARY SCOTT WHITE has written three novels, *The Square Root of Fun, The Wrong Detective,* and more recently, *Dunwoody,* all of which are unpublished. He has also written poetry. A former Tallahasseean, he lives and works in London, England.

MICHAEL CUNNINGHAM is the author of *A Home at the End of the World* (Farrar Straus Giroux). His fiction has appeared in *The New Yorker* and other magazines. He lives in New York City.

GARY INDIANA has been a weekly arts columnist for *The Village Voice* since 1985; in addition, he contributes to a number of publications — among them, *Artforum, Art in America, HG,* and *Bomb*—and is the author of *Scar Tissue,* a collection of short stories, and *Horse Crazy,* his first novel. He lives and works in New York City.

EILEEN MYLES's new book of poems called *Not Me* is just out from Semiotext(e). Her collections of stories, *Bread & Water* and *1969,* are published by Hanuman Books. She also writes for *Art in America, The Village Voice* and *Outweek.* She lives and works in New York City.

LYNNE TILLMAN is a New York-based writer and filmmaker. She is the author of *Haunted Houses, Absence Makes the Heart,* and *Motion Sickness.* With artists Kiki Smith and Jane Dickson, she collaborated on *Madame Realism* and *Living with Contradictions,* respectively. She is also the co-director and writer of the independent feature film, *Committed.* Her criticism on art, film and literature appears in *Art in America, Artforum, The New York Timee Book Review* and *The Village Voice.*

PATRICK McGRATH is the author of *Blood and Water and Other Tales* and *The Grotesque. Spider* is his latest novel. He lives in New York City.

WENDY WALKER was born in 1951. Her volume of tales, *The Sea Rabbit, or, The Artist of Life* was published by Sun and Moon Press. Forthcoming from Sun and Moon (Summer 1991) is a novel, *The Secret Service.* She is currently at work on a 'historical' novel. She lives and works in New York City.

ABOUT THE EDITORS

PATRICIA COLLINS and RICHARD MILAZZO have worked collaboratively as curators and critics in the New York art world and internationally since 1982.

In the 1970's, Richard Milazzo co-founded Out of London Press, among which publications he co-edited the first English translation of *Pontormo's Diary* (1979). From 1982 to 1984, Collins & Milazzo founded and edited *Effects: Magazine for New Art Theory*, and in 1984 they curated their first exhibitions, including a major exhibition of New York art at Florida State University, Tallahassee, Florida. Since then, they have curated over 40 exhibitions throughout the United States and Europe, among which the most recent are *Pre-Pop Post-Appropriation*, in cooperation with Leo Castelli, *Art at the End of the Social* (the Rooseum, Malmö, Sweden), *The Last Decade: American Artists of the 80's* (Tony Shafrazi Gallery, N.Y.) and *Who Framed Modern Art or the Quantitative Life of Roger Rabbit* (Sidney Janis Gallery, N.Y.). Too numerous to list here, their exhibitions have included such artists as Picasso, Duchamp, Brancusi, Giacometti, De Kooning, Pollock, Rauschenberg, Johns, Warhol, Twombly and Stella.

In 1985, Collins & Milazzo were appointed Senior Critics in the Department of Sculpture at Yale University. The lectures at Yale, entitled *Hyperframes: A Post-Appropriation Discourse in Art*, are currently being published in three volumes by Éditions Antoine Candau, Paris, France.

Collins & Milazzo's critical and curatorial work originally fashioned the theoretical context for the new Conceptual Art that rose to prominence in the late 1980's in New York. It was through their exhibitions and writings that the work of many of the artists associated with this kind of art was first brought together—artists such as Ross Bleckner, Allan McCollum, Peter Halley, Jeff Koons, Jonathan Lasker, Gary Stephan, Philip Taaffe, Haim Steinbach, Annette Lemieux, Saint Clair Cemin, Sal Scarpitta, Mike and Doug Starn, Robert Gober, Suzan Etkin and Meg Webster, among others.

Among their many publications, forthcoming is a book of essays they are editing, *Outside America: Essays on the State of Contemporary Art and Culture*, which includes texts by artists, writers, critics, historians and philosophers, such as Peter Sloterdijk, Greil Marcus, Peter Halley, Barbara Kruger, Gary Indiana, Gianni Vattimo, Craig Adcock and Peter Fend.

RIDGEFIELD PRESS is a non-profit organization based in Talla-hassee, Florida, and New York, dedicated to publishing books in the fields of literature, art, art crticism and the various crafts. Modeling itself after The Hogarth Press, founded by Virginia Woolf and the Bloomsbury group in London in 1917, as well as the Arts and Crafts movement led by Gustav Stickley in America (which was begun in nineteenth century England by such artists and philosopher-critics as John Ruskin and William Morris), it is the intention of RIDGEFIELD PRESS to create a distinguished link between the practical and the intellectual, the aesthetical and the social, and between local and international culture.

RIDGEFIELD PRESS was founded and is edited by Patricia Collins and Richard Milazzo. RIDGEFIELD PRESS is located at 217 S. Adams Street, Tallahassee, Florida 32302, and 99 Spring Street, New York, NY 10012.

FORTHCOMING TITLES

Bonnie Williams, *Zone 9: Gardening in the Lower Middle South*